SO, WHAT'S THE BOOK ALL ABOUT...

Three women. One unforgettable Spanish summer. And a secret that will change everything.

When Maria, Rosie and Emma met in their fifties—newly divorced, widowed or bravely single—they never imagined how quickly strangers could become the family you choose. So when their friend passes away, there's only one way to honour her memory: a trip to Majorca to scatter her ashes in the place she loved most.

But what begins as a bittersweet farewell soon turns into the adventure of a lifetime. Beneath the island's blazing skies and cobbled streets, Maria finds herself drawn to a gentle Spanish historian with a past as tangled as her own. Rosie, irrepressible as ever, tumbles into an unexpected romance that makes her question everything she thought she wanted. And Emma, quiet and tentative, finally steps into the creative life she never dared to claim.

As they follow a trail of secrets, the women discover that love can come at any age, that endings can be disguised as beginnings, and that sometimes the bravest thing you'll ever do is choose happiness.

Set against golden beaches, hidden alleys and endless glasses of Rioja, *Sassy Señoritas* is a heartwarming, life-affirming novel about friendship found later in life, second chances, and the courage to start over—no matter when you begin.

Perfect for fans of Marian Keyes, Jojo Moyes and anyone who believes it's never too late to follow your heart...

SASSY SENORITAS

SASSY AND SIXTY

BERNICE BLOOM

A QUICK REMINDER ABOUT WHAT HAPPENED IN THE LAST BOOK...

*P*reviously in Sassy Sisterhood...
When Rosie, Emma, Lisa and Maria moved into their grand Victorian house in Esher, they thought they were sharing bills and bathrooms. They had no idea they were also signing up for midnight ghost hunts, medical mysteries, emotional confessions, haunted history, and a whole lot of wine.

From day one, the house buzzed with life and chaos. Lisa, glamorous and guarded, turned heads and dropped hints about a mysterious illness. Emma, all mud-splattered boots and mischief, stirred up stories from her scandalous past (including a secret cleaner in the wardrobe). Maria, the practical one, uncovered shocking truths about the house's previous residents – poisonings! Ghosts! Victorian scandal! And Rosie? She juggled dating drama (Mike, we're looking at you), grandparent duties (prostitutes and dirty car films were involved – don't ask), and her trademark eyebrow of doom.

Together, they survived nosy neighbours, demanding children, rogue politicians, and the occasional spectral disturbance – all while building something scarce: a chosen family of women who lift each other up.

But then Lisa fell ill. At first, they all tried to pretend it was nothing – just another chapter in the drama. But it wasn't. Her decline was swift and devastating. And when she died, it was as if the laughter in the house dimmed overnight. Losing Lisa left a silence none of them knew how to fill.

Now they're off to Majorca to scatter Lisa's ashes – but with secrets still lingering, passions on the horizon, and flamenco dancers in their future, the adventure is only just beginning.

THE TAXI RIDE FROM HELL

"*M*y God, I hate my hands. They are deeply unpleasant to look at," said Rosie, holding them up and studying them like she'd never seen hands before. "They're the sort of dried-out, wrinkly things that my grandma had. And before anyone mentions it - yes, I know I am a granny now, but I don't want the gnarled mitts to go with it."

"No one over the age of 60 has nice hands," said Emma, reflecting on her own. "They've done too much. Seen too much. Carried too much."

"Yeah, but mine are particularly bad. I look like I'm wearing nude gloves that are too big for me and puckered around the knuckle," said Rosie.

Maria smiled wistfully. "Mine used to be so slender and delicate. Now they look like they could shovel coal."

The taxi carrying the three women and their six wrinkly old hands wound through the Tramuntana mountains, passing ancient olive groves that sat next to stone terraces, built centuries ago. Ahead were mountains and whitewashed villages dotted in distant valleys.

Three hours ago, they'd been in England, where summer was

still crawling out of hibernation. Here, the Mediterranean sun attacked the car's roof like it was wielding a baseball bat.

"I'm too old for this level of heat," said Maria, her ugly old hands temporarily forgotten as she moved to the side, peeling her thighs from the vinyl seat with a sound like Velcro being ripped apart. "Did you hear that? I'm melting into the upholstery. Someone will have to scrape me off it by the time we get there."

Emma fanned herself with a crumpled tourist map. "It's like being back in the menopause again."

Maria gasped at Emma's reckless use of the 'm' word, while Rosie reached out a sweaty hand towards her friend, their fingers sticking together like overcooked pasta. "Nothing is as bad as being back in the menopause again."

The taxi driver, seemingly immune to the heat in his long-sleeved shirt, glanced at them in the rearview mirror. "Beautifulist day, yes? Perfection for sighting sees!" He had the cheerfulness of someone who regularly watched tourists dissolve into puddles of sunscreen and regret. "You like nice suns?"

"Oh yes," they all replied, their faces pink and hot while rivulets of sweat ran down their backs. They'd never been so uncomfortable; they hated the soaring temperatures, but eager not to offend, they smiled warmly at the friendly foreigner. "The sun is very nice."

Rosie checked her watch. "We're much later than we thought we'd be. It took us ages to get through the airport."

"Hopefully we'll get there soon," said Maria. "I've written a list of everything we need to try and get done today, and we're falling way behind schedule."

"Ladies, please!" Emma removed her oversized sunglasses with the solemnity of a judge passing sentence. "We're in Majorca! Land of passion and possibility! Let's drink sangria, flamenco dance, and eat paella till we burst. No need for checking watches or making plans."

Usually, Rosie would have agreed, it wasn't a holiday if it came with time constraints. But this trip was different. Their lovely friend Lisa had died six months previously, leaving them all bereft. She was a beautiful, bright, vivacious woman - talented and gorgeous in equal measure.

Months before her death, the four of them had moved into a big house together. They were starting over...leaving divorces, grown-up children and errant husbands aside to begin a life of female friendship and inappropriate levels of alcohol consumption. Losing Lisa had hit them all hard. Lisa wasn't meant to die. She was too lovely for something as mundane as dying.

After her death, the women discovered four photographs that she'd left behind. Lisa had asked that a quarter of her ashes be scattered in each of the locations shown in the pictures. The search for the location of the final image had brought them to Majorca on this sweltering summer's day.

Rosie pulled out the photograph and studied it. Emma and Maria leaned over to look at it, too. They'd looked at the picture a thousand times but still found it captivating...their beautiful friend, smiling, frozen in time. She stood beside a door painted the colour of the sky, her dark hair loose around her shoulders. Half-visible beside her was another figure, an arm draped casually around Lisa's waist, fingers splayed possessively against her hip.

Underneath lay the caption: *Majorca. Where my true story began.*

Where my true story began. What did that mean?

The women knew that Lisa had been adopted as a baby. One of their final acts when she was alive was to find her birth mother. But very little was known about Lisa's early life, those precious few years after she was adopted. They had no idea whether she was taken to Spain straight away, as a baby, or later as a young child. They had no idea whether she went to school in Spain or in England. How would they find all this information out, and trace the location featured in the photograph with so few clues to go on?

"Why is quiet in car. No chatty now?" said the cab driver, a man with the magnificent moustache of a retired matador. He had introduced himself earlier with a flourish and a gold-toothed grin. "My name Antonio. Sometimes I called Tony. Yes, I am Tony Taxi." Now he was staring at them with a fascination usually reserved for exotic zoo animals.

"Primera vez en Majorca?" he asked.

"Sí," Emma replied, exhausting approximately one-third of her Spanish vocabulary in a single syllable without really understanding what he'd asked.

He nodded sagely. "Es mágico," he said, tapping his heart.

"It's magic!" said Emma. "See - I can speak Spanish."

The road curved, and suddenly, there it was.

"Deià. Mira qué hermoso lugar. ¿No es maravilloso?"

They were all so captivated by the sight of the beautiful place in front of them that they didn't hear what the driver said. He repeated himself, and continued to chat in Spanish, but they were still none the wiser.

"I think he's asking if we're nuns," Rosie announced, her damp hair flat against her head, as she turned to beam at Tony the Taxi.

Maria was the only one of them who spoke Spanish. She pulled her phrase book out of her bag and flicked through it. She may be the only woman in the western world still using a phrase book, but she didn't care - phones were for phoning, not translating. "He's not asking if we're nuns, Rosie. He's asking where we're from."

"No, definitely nuns. Look at his face."

"¿De dónde son ustedes?" he said, his voice rich with curiosity and something that might have been concern.

Maria looked up from her phrasebook. "Come on - one of

you must know how to say England in Spanish? You can't leave me to do all the work."

"Inglaterra," Emma said mildly, adding another line to her sketch of the coastline. She was determined to use her time on this trip to Majorca to work on her art. She'd been to art school many years ago but had abandoned it for a more lucrative career and never quite gone back. As the years passed, she found she missed it.

"If you're wondering how I know the Spanish for England, it's because I watched the Eurovision Song Contest when it was held in Liverpool, and all the juries opened with 'Hello England.'. I know how to say 'England' in every Eurovision accent."

"Eurovision? That's quite a confession, you dark horse!" Rosie laughed, then leaned towards Antonio with renewed enthusiasm. "Inglaterra! We're from Inglaterra!"

Antonio's face lit up like Christmas morning. "¡Inglaterra! ¡Muy bien! ¡The Beatles! ¡Fish and chips!"

"Yes, yes, exactly!" Rosie clapped her hands together. "Though personally, I'm more of a Rolling Stones girl."

The taxi swerved slightly as Antonio twisted around to look at her with approval. "¡Mick Jagger! ¡Muy sexy!"

"Oh, you charmer." Rosie actually giggled-a sound Maria hadn't heard from her friend in months. Not since Lisa's funeral, when they'd all stood around making polite conversation about church flowers while their hearts broke quietly in their chests.

With the sound of Rosie's laughter, Maria felt something tight in her chest begin to loosen. Maybe this mad adventure would work. Maybe they could find where Lisa belonged, and maybe-just maybe-they could remember how to enjoy life again in the process.

"Antonio," she said, leaning forward with sudden determination. "Tenemos una foto." She pulled the worn photograph from her handbag-Lisa at twenty, radiant and mysterious, standing beside that damned blue door that had haunted their dreams for weeks. "¿Conoces este lugar?"

Antonio's eyes widened as he glanced at the photo, then back at the road, then at the photo again. The taxi slowed considerably as his attention was divided between driving and staring at the image.

"¡Dios mío!" he breathed, his voice dropping to something approaching reverence. "Esta chica... muy bonita. ¿Es su hermana?"

"He's asking if she's our sister," Maria translated quietly.

Maria's throat tightened. "Our friend. Era nuestra amiga. She... she died."

The change in Antonio was immediate. His face softened, and he crossed himself quickly before taking the photo with gentle hands. He studied it for a long moment while the taxi coasted along the sun-dappled road.

"Esta puerta..." he said finally, pointing at the blue door. "Yo la conozco. Not where, but..." He struggled with English, his face scrunched in concentration. "Muy importante. For niños. Children."

The three women exchanged glances.

"Children?" Maria repeated.

"Sí, sí. Niños pequeños." Antonio made a rocking motion with his arms. "Babies. Before, many years." He handed the photo back carefully, as if it were made of glass. "My abuela, she work there. Long time ago."

Emma had stopped sketching entirely.

"His grandmother worked somewhere with children? That's what it sounds like."

She turned back to Antonio. "I'm afraid I can't really understand that."

"Si," he replied.

Antonio caught the sombreness that had settled over his

passengers, so with the intuitive kindness that seemed to be encoded in Spanish DNA, he decided to try and cheer them up. He reached over and turned up the radio. Gentle guitar music filled the car, something warm and hopeful that wrapped around them like a promise.

"No worrying," he said, meeting Maria's eyes in the rearview mirror. "We find. In Majorca, we help always." He grinned again, that gold tooth catching the light. "Especially for ladies who love lots the Rolling Stoners."

Rosie burst into laughter despite herself. "I think I'm going to like it here."

Outside the taxi windows, Majorca unfolded beautifully. Now they were closer to the white buildings, they could see how gorgeous they were, on hillsides looking down towards an impossibly blue sea, bougainvillaea spilling over ancient stone walls in fountains of purple and pink.

"You know what?" Maria said, stuffing her phrase book back into her bag. "I think Lisa would have loved this."

"Are you kidding?" Rosie twisted around to grin at her friends. "She's probably orchestrating the whole thing from her big throne in heaven...looking down and thinking 'right, let's get them a completely bonkers driver who can't speak a word of English...that should start things off nicely for them...'

Antonio, following perhaps half the conversation but all of the emotional undercurrents, nodded sagely. "Your friend in heaven, she have good spirit. I feel much it." He tapped his chest over his heart. "Here. She with you now in taxi car with Tony Taxi."

He rounded a curve, and suddenly their villa came into view-a sprawling building in white, like so many of those they had seen along the way, with blue shutters and a terrace that seemed to hang suspended above the Mediterranean, in the western foothills of the Tramuntana mountains. It wasn't the pristine luxury they'd been promised on the website, but it was something better. It looked like the kind of place where adventures began.

"¡Llegamos!" Antonio announced, pulling into the gravel drive with a flourish. "You are home please!"

As they climbed out of the taxi, legs stiff from the journey, Maria realised that for the first time in months, she was excited about tomorrow. Whatever came next, wrong turns, language barriers, wild goose chases, or blessed discoveries, they would face it together. As they tipped their driver generously and enjoyed his celebratory dance, they all knew that the adventure had officially begun.

VILLA SURPRISE

*T*he front door key turned with a grudging resistance that suggested it hadn't been used recently. Or possibly ever.

"Are we sure this is the right place?" Maria asked, wrestling with the ancient lock while Rosie peered through grimy windows and Emma photographed a lizard sunning itself on the doorframe.

"Villa Rosa Blanca," Rosie read from the faded ceramic plaque beside the door. "Either this is it, or we're about to become very unwelcome guests."

The door finally surrendered with a dramatic groan, swinging open to reveal... well, certainly not the Mediterranean paradise promised on the rental website.

"Oh," said Maria.

"My," said Emma.

"God," finished Rosie.

The entrance hall stretched before them in all its 1970s glory-orange shag carpet that had seen better decades, wallpaper featuring psychedelic pineapples, and a chandelier apparently constructed from a disco ball and a fishing net.

"I think," Emma said carefully, setting down her suitcase, "that the photographs on the website must have been taken with a very forgiving camera."

"And possibly by someone who was legally blind," Rosie added, but she was grinning. "Like we said before, this is all Lisa's doing. She is howling with laughter somewhere."

The sitting room continued the theme with enthusiasm. Junk shop furniture sprawled across terracotta tiles. A lime green sofa from the eighties faced off against armour (or at least a very convincing replica), while a coffee table made from drift-wood supported a lamp shaped like a flamingo.

"It's certainly... eclectic," Maria ventured.

"It's horrific," Emma said, then immediately looked guilty. "I mean, in a charming way."

"Are you kidding?" Rosie threw herself onto the lime green sofa, which received her with a wheeze of ancient springs. "This is exactly what we need. Look at this place-it's impossible to be serious here. It's like being inside a kaleidoscope designed by someone having a very cheerful nervous breakdown."

She had a point. The villa seemed to radiate a kind of determined joy, as if someone had decided that if life was going to be ridiculous, it might as well be spectacularly ridiculous.

Maria wandered towards the kitchen, drawn by curiosity and the faint sound of dripping. The room she discovered was a masterpiece of creative plumbing and optimistic electrical work. The refrigerator hummed with the determination of a small aircraft engine, the cooker appeared to be held together with prayer and electrical tape, and the tap dripped with the persistence of a woodpecker relentlessly tapping at the bark of a tree.

"Ladies," she called, "I think we may need to adjust our expectations about home cooking."

"That's what restaurants are for," Rosie called back. "Come look at this!"

Maria found her friends standing at the glass doors that led to the terrace, and suddenly the villa's shortcomings became irrelevant. The view beyond was so beautiful that it made her chest ache.

The terrace stretched out over lush gardens where lemon trees heavy with fruit competed for space with wild rosemary and lavender. Beyond that, there were olive groves and a sea so blue it looked like someone had spilt liquid sapphire across the horizon. The late afternoon sun turned everything golden, and the air carried the scent of pine and salt and something indefinably warm that might have been happiness itself.

"Oh," Maria breathed.

"Now I understand," Emma said softly. "This is why people fall in love with islands."

"This is why people fall in love, period," Rosie added, then laughed at her own romantic nonsense.

They stood in comfortable silence for a moment, letting the beauty wash over them. Then Emma disappeared and returned with a bottle of wine she'd excavated from their bag of pre-flight purchases along with three mismatched glasses from the kitchen.

"To Lisa," she said simply, pouring wine that caught the light like liquid fire.

"To Lisa," Maria and Rosie echoed.

They carried their glasses to the terrace, where weathered wicker furniture waited under a vine-covered pergola. Maria pulled out the photograph and propped it against a terra cotta pot filled with geraniums. In the Mediterranean light, Lisa looked even more radiant.

"So," Rosie said, settling back in her chair with the contentment of a cat in sunshine, "tomorrow we start hunting for blue doors."

"Antonio seemed to think he recognised something about the photo," Emma mused. "Something about children."

"I don't think he knew what he was talking about," said Maria.

"No, too excited by the idea of the Rolling Stoners," said Rosie.

Maria smiled to herself, "Lisa never talked much about being adopted. I wonder now if that was because talking about before was too painful, or because she genuinely didn't remember much."

Emma nodded. "It's hard to be sure. We don't know anything about her life here or when she returned to England. In fact, when I think about it-as I have endlessly since she died, she never spoke about her past much at all. As far as I was concerned, she was a brilliant and beautiful writer and a fabulous friend; I never thought about all she'd been through. We all met so late in life that we just don't know much about each other as children and young women."

"Maybe being here will help us understand what happened before she became the Lisa we knew. We'll find out all the things she couldn't tell us herself," said Rosie.

The three women lifted their wine and made a toast to their friend, looking out across the stunning vista as they did. As if summoned by their gesture, a peacock strutted across the garden below them with all the swaggering confidence of a twenty-year-old who'd spent an hour perfecting his hair and was absolutely certain he was the best-looking thing on two legs. His tail fanned in a magnificent display, clearly expecting applause for his sheer fabulousness.

"Well, hello, gorgeous," Rosie said appreciatively. "Someone's not suffering from low self-esteem."

"He's magnificent," Emma breathed. "Look at the way he moves, like he owns the entire island."

"Did anyone else know there would be peacocks?" Maria asked, still staring at the theatrical display below. "I didn't know they had them here."

"Oh, it seems they have everything here...like pineapple wallpaper, for example," Rosie countered. "No one expected that."

The sun was beginning to set, and somewhere in the distance, church bells chimed the hour; the sound carried on the warm evening air.

"I can't remember the last time I felt this relaxed," Maria admitted, surprising herself with the admission.

"That's because you've been wound tighter than a spring for months," Rosie said gently. "We all have. It's hard to relax when your heart is breaking."

"Hearts heal," Emma added quietly. "Lisa would want ours to heal."

"She'd also want us to have completely inappropriate adventures with charming Spanish men," Rosie said, raising her glass. "So, here's to inappropriate adventures."

"And charming Spanish men," Emma agreed with a grin.

"And finding our friend's blue door," Maria added.

They clinked glasses as the first stars appeared in the darkening sky.

"You know what?" said Emma, topping up their glasses with the last of the wine. "I think this is going to be the adventure of our lives."

"It better be," Rosie said with a wicked grin. "We're not getting any younger."

"Speak for yourself," Emma said mildly. "I'm planning to go full Benjamin Button any day now"

"In that case," Maria said, raising her glass one more time, "here's to getting better with time."

The peacock called from somewhere in the gathering dusk, a sound that was both absurd and oddly majestic, and the three women dissolved into laughter that carried across the terrace and out into the Majorcan night.

Tomorrow, Maria thought as she watched the stars appear,

they would begin their search and, whatever it took, they would find the blue door.

THREE WOMEN AND A BUS
CALLED ROSA

*T*heir first morning in the apartment came with all the subtlety of a brass band falling downstairs. A rooster crowed, church bells rang out, and the villa's plumbing clattered and banged.

"Is that the shower or a small earthquake?" Rosie called from the bathroom, her voice barely audible over the sound of pipes having a nervous breakdown.

"Both, I think," Maria replied, wrestling unsuccessfully with the coffee machine. "How's the water pressure?"

"What water pressure? It's like being misted by a plant sprayer."

Emma emerged from her room looking remarkably put-together for someone who had navigated the same bathroom challenges earlier that morning. Her hair was damp but tidy.

"There's a trick to the shower," she said serenely. "You have to turn the taps in a specific sequence while standing on one foot and humming something Spanish."

"You're joking," Maria said.

"Only about the hopping and humming parts."

The coffee machine finally surrendered and produced something that was technically coffee, though it bore only a passing resemblance to anything they'd previously encountered. Maria poured three cups then sat down to consult her carefully prepared list. She'd googled 'tourist attractions on Majorca' before leaving, then had gone through the list and identified those which had blue doors. It wasn't the most sophisticated of approaches, but it had left her with two obvious ones to try and a list of others that were possible. Once they had found the right door, they would arrange to come back the following day and scatter the ashes at a nearby location.

"Right," she said, spreading a map across the flamingo-shaped coffee table. "I've identified many possible locations in Palma alone. We can start with the cathedral, then work our way through the old town, checking off—"

"Or," Rosie interrupted, appearing in a sundress that would have been conservative on a twenty-year-old but was delightfully scandalous on a woman of sixty-three, "we could wander around and see what happens."

"See what happens is not a plan, Rosie."

"Sometimes it's the best plan."

Emma sat cross-legged on the lime green sofa. "Half the joy of travel is getting lost."

"Half the joy of travel is not spending three days wandering in circles. We need to find the blue door. Once we know where that is, we can relax a bit. This is for Lisa, remember," Maria countered, but she was smiling. The truth was, she felt lighter this morning than she had in months.

They compromised, as they always did. Maria's list would provide structure, but they agreed to be open to detours, distractions, and what Rosie termed "delicious serendipity."

The bus ride into Palma proved to be their first adventure. What Maria's guidebook had described as "reliable local transport" was a mobile festival. Their driver, a woman who introduced herself as Rosa with the theatrical flair of someone walking onto the stage at Wembley, knew everyone who boarded. She dispensed advice, gossip, and what appeared to be relationship counselling in rapid-fire Spanish while navigating traffic with the casual confidence of someone playing a video game. She promised to let the women know when it was their stop.

"She's magnificent," Rosie whispered, watching Rosa gesture animatedly at a passenger who was having romantic difficulties.

"I want to be her when I grow up."

"You're already grown up," Emma pointed out.

"That's a minor detail," Rosie replied. "My plan still stands. Look at her—she's chatting away, navigating traffic that would terrify a Formula One driver, and somehow managing to make everyone on this bus feel like they're part of her extended family."

"She does seem to know everyone," Maria observed, watching Rosa blow a kiss to an elderly man getting off at the market stop while simultaneously scolding a teenager for not giving up his seat to a pregnant woman.

"That's what I want," Rosie said wistfully. "To be the kind of person who makes everything around them more alive just by existing."

"You already are that person," Emma said softly. "You just don't see it."

The bus wound through narrow streets designed for donkeys rather than modern transportation, past balconies covered in the morning's washing. Through the windows, Maria caught glimpses of daily life unfolding—elderly men playing chess in tiny squares, children chasing footballs through courtyards, women hanging laundry while calling out gossip to their neighbours.

"It's like living inside a postcard," Emma murmured.

"A postcard where everyone lives real lives," Rosie added. "Not just poses for tourists."

When they finally reached the cathedral stop, Rosa turned to them with a motherly smile.

"Cathedral, yes? You want this stop? Very beautiful, but very busy with tourists. You want real Palma, you walk the small streets behind. More authentic, less cameras."

"Gracias, Rosa," Maria said, attempting her careful Spanish.

"De nada, guapas."

Palma Cathedral rose before them like something from a fever dream, all Gothic spires and rose windows that caught the morning light like captured rainbows. The sheer scale of it made them feel like ants approaching a monument built by giants, its honey-coloured stone walls soaring toward a sky so blue it looked painted.

"Good Lord," Maria breathed, craning her neck to take in the full height of the bell towers before watching the steady stream of visitors flowing through the entrance.

They approached the blue doors that Maria had identified in her research—magnificent oak portals studded with iron hinges that had probably been forged by medieval craftsmen who understood that some things were meant to last forever.

"These are spectacular," Emma said, running her fingers along the carved stonework that framed the entrance, "but they're absolutely nothing like the door in Lisa's photograph."

Maria held up the small picture, comparing it to the cathedral's imposing entrance. The difference was immediately obvious—these doors belonged to a building designed to inspire awe and demonstrate the power of faith. Lisa's door was something altogether more humble.

"Too grand," Emma continued, shaking her head. "Lisa's door was simpler. More... domestic."

"Domestic," Maria repeated, making a note in her careful handwriting. "Good point. This looks like somewhere you'd go to confess your sins to God. Lisa's door looks like somewhere you'd go to confess your secrets to a friend."

"So we're looking for somewhere more human-scaled," Rosie concluded, studying the photograph over Maria's shoulder. "Somewhere that was built for living in, not worshipping in."

"Rosa was right about the small streets," Emma said, gesturing toward the maze of narrow alleys that branched off from the cathedral square. "Maybe we should follow her advice and see what real Palma looks like."

"We will," Maria said, consulting her list with the determined efficiency of a general planning a campaign. "But let's check off the obvious tourist spots first—that way we'll know for certain we're not missing something simple."

She pulled out a small notebook. "On to the Museo de Mallorca. It's only a ten-minute walk according to my research, and then we can explore Rosa's 'real Palma' with clear consciences."

"Your research," Rosie observed fondly, "puts the Spanish Inquisition to shame for thoroughness."

"There's nothing wrong with being methodical," Maria replied.

They wound through streets that grew progressively narrower and more atmospheric, past shops selling everything from handmade lace to suspiciously tourist-friendly 'authentic' Spanish guitars.

The morning was warming up, and the combination of Emma's artistic eye, Rosie's commentary on the passing pedestrians, and Maria's navigation created a comfortable rhythm of friendship and exploration.

"That man," Rosie said, nodding discreetly toward a gentleman in an immaculate white suit walking a tiny dog wearing what appeared to be a bow tie, "is either very sophisticated or completely mad."

"Can't he be both?" Emma asked.

"In Spain, I think that's practically a requirement," Maria said, checking her map again. "Ah, here we are."

The Museo de Mallorca sat quietly behind its blue door like a modest cousin of the cathedral—impressive in its own right, but without the soaring ambition of its religious neighbour. The building was classical and dignified, with the kind of weathered stone that spoke of centuries of Balearic sunshine and the occasional Mediterranean storm.

Maria held up Lisa's photograph again, and they studied both doors with the intensity of art critics examining a masterpiece. The museum's blue door was certainly blue—a deep, historical blue that probably had an official name like "Royal Mediterranean" or "Heritage Azure." It was set in an archway designed by someone who understood proportion and dignity. Bronze plaques announced the museum's credentials in three languages, and everything about the entrance suggested serious cultural endeavours and respectful contemplation of the island's past.

"It's beautiful," Emma said diplomatically.

"It's completely wrong," Rosie said more directly. "It's certainly closer, but wrong."

Maria compared the photograph one more time, then sighed and made another note in her book.

"The proportions are different, the stonework is different, even the way the light falls is different."

"Plus," Emma added, studying Lisa's photograph more carefully, "look at the ground in front of Lisa's door. It's not paved stones like this—it looks more like tiles or something. Can you see?"

"So we're looking for somewhere quite smart?" Maria said, her organisational mind already recategorising their search parameters.

"I don't think so, not necessarily. A lot of houses had tiles. I don't think it means anything," said Rosie.

"Come on," Emma pointed towards a tiny café tucked between two tourist shops like a secret only locals were supposed to know about.

The narrow frontage was easy to miss—just a hand-painted sign that read "Café" in faded blue letters, and a doorway barely wide enough for two people to pass.

"Let's go in here. I need caffeine before we tackle any more monumental blue doors."

The interior was delightfully cramped, with perhaps eight small tables crowded together under a ceiling so low that anyone over six feet would need to duck. Mismatched chairs surrounded tables that wobbled charmingly, and the walls were covered with a collection of photographs that appeared to document every significant moment in the neighbourhood's history for the past fifty years.

"This is perfect," Rosie said, settling into a chair that creaked welcomingly. "Authentic, atmospheric, and completely free of other tourists."

"I feel like we've stumbled into someone's living room," Maria said, looking around at the family photographs and what appeared to be several generations of local football trophies.

The owner emerged from behind a counter —a weathered man with kind eyes and the sort of comfortable belly that suggested he sampled his own cooking regularly. Without being asked, he brought them three small glasses of water and began preparing cortados with the practised movements of someone who had been making coffee since before any of them were born.

"Gracias," Maria said carefully, attempting to deploy her phrase-book Spanish.

"De nada," he replied with a smile that transformed his entire face. "English, yes? You are looking for something in Palma?"

"Blue doors," Emma said, pulling out Lisa's photograph. "We're on a sort of treasure hunt."

"Treasure hunt!" Rosie laughed, raising her cortado in a mock toast. "That makes us sound much more adventurous than 'three middle-aged women wandering around with a mysterious photograph.'"

"Speak for yourself," Maria protested. "I prefer 'three sophisticated travellers pursuing cultural research.'"

"With a mysterious photograph," Emma added solemnly.

"That we found in a dead woman's effects," Rosie continued.

"Stop," Maria said, giggling despite herself. "You're making us sound like the beginning of a very peculiar detective novel."

"The Case of the Curious Blue Door," Emma suggested.

"Featuring three unlikely heroines," Rosie added dramatically, "armed only with determination, dubious Spanish, and one questionable hat."

"What's wrong with my hat?" asked Maria.

"Nothing. It's adorable. We're just being silly," said Emma.

Their laughter filled the small space, and the café owner watched with obvious pleasure, clearly enjoying their English humour even if he didn't understand all the words.

"Blue doors, yes," he said, studying Lisa's photograph with interest. "Many blue doors in Palma. This one..." He squinted at the image, turning it slightly in the light. "This is not tourist place, I think. This is more... how you say... residential? Family place?"

"That's what we're beginning to suspect," Maria said. "We've tried the cathedral and the museum, and they're both too grand."

"Too official," Emma agreed.

"My mother," the café owner said suddenly, his face brightening with inspiration, "she reads palms—"

She knows many stories about Palma, many old places. You like she looks at your photograph? Maybe she knows this door."

"I would love to have my palm read in Palma. This day just keeps getting better and better,"

Before anyone could protest, an elderly woman emerged from the back room like a fortune-telling force of nature, moving with the purposeful energy of someone who had been reading palms since before any of them were born. She was tiny but commanding, dressed entirely in black except for a collection of silver bracelets that jangled musically with every gesture. Her eyes were dark and sharp, missing nothing as she surveyed the three friends with obvious curiosity.

Without preamble, she seized Maria's hand and began studying it with the intensity of a scholar examining an ancient manuscript. Her weathered fingers traced the lines of Maria's palm while she muttered what sounded like a running commentary in rapid Spanish, occasionally clicking her tongue in what might have been disapproval or surprise.

"Abuela says your heart line is very interesting," the son translated, looking slightly embarrassed by his mother's directness. "She says you have been hiding from love."

"I haven't been hiding," Maria protested. "I've been... taking a break."

The elderly woman looked up at Maria with raised eyebrows and delivered what was clearly a lecture, complete with finger-wagging and gestures towards Maria's chest.

"She says your heart has been sleeping like a bear in winter," the son continued, "but Spain will wake it up. She sees romance coming from an unexpected direction—someone who makes you laugh when you think you should be serious."

"Well, that's encouraging."

The fortune teller wasn't finished. She pointed at something in Maria's palm and spoke more urgently, her voice rising with excitement.

"She also sees... a door?" The son looked confused by his

translation. "A blue door that will bring you answers about the past and possibilities for the future."

Maria's eyes widened. "Did she say that, or are you making that up?"

"I swear on my mother's cooking," he replied solemnly. "She says the door you seek is connected to your heart's awakening. They are part of the same story."

The old woman released Maria's hand and immediately seized Rosie's, examining it with equal intensity. This palm reading involved considerably more dramatic gestures and what sounded like gentle scolding.

"She says you," the son translated with obvious embarrassment, "have too many admirers and must choose wisely. Your heart is generous, but sometimes too trusting."

"Too many admirers?" Emma asked innocently. "Is that actually a problem people have?"

"It's a terrible burden," Rosie said solemnly. "The responsibility of managing all that adoration. Very taxing."

The fortune teller continued her examination, tracing lines and muttering appreciatively. She seemed to approve of what she saw in Rosie's palm, nodding and patting her hand encouragingly.

"She also says that you flirt with danger, but it keeps life interesting," the son continued, looking even more uncomfortable.

"Only on weekdays," Rosie replied cheerfully. "I take weekends off."

"And that you will help a friend find something precious that was lost."

"Lost like misplaced, or lost like forgotten?" Rosie asked with interest.

More rapid Spanish followed, with the old woman gesturing towards the photograph that lay on their table.

"Lost like... hidden?" the son offered uncertainly. "She says you have the gift of seeing what others miss, especially when it comes to matters of the heart."

Finally, the fortune teller turned to Emma's palm and immediately brightened, chattering excitedly while tracing lines with obvious delight. Her entire demeanour changed, becoming almost maternal as she examined Emma's hand.

"She says you have artist's hands," the translation came, "but you don't trust your own gifts. She sees great talent waiting to emerge with... feeling? Understanding?"

"What kind of understanding?" Emma asked nervously.

The old woman looked directly into Emma's eyes as her son spoke slowly, as if ensuring his mother's words would be remembered.

"She says you will discover a talent you didn't know you had —something that will surprise everyone, including yourself. And she says you will dance."

"I don't dance," Emma said firmly.

"Everyone dances," the fortune teller replied in suddenly perfect English, patting Emma's hand with obvious affection. "Some people just haven't found the right music yet."

She stood up then, apparently finished with her mystical consultations, and disappeared back into the depths of the café as suddenly as she had appeared.

"Well," Rosie said after a moment of stunned silence, "that was either the most accurate fortune telling I've ever experienced, or your mother is an excellent judge of character."

"Both," the son said with a grin. "She's been reading palms for sixty years. She sees things."

"OK, we must go now. We need to search for this blue door."

"You must try The Centro Cultural San Miguel, just here..." He pointed to a large building across the street. "They very help you."

THE HISTORIAN WITH
KIND EYES

*T*he Centro Cultural San Miguel looked like the sort of place that existed by accident...tucked between a pharmacy that sold suspiciously green remedies and a shop devoted entirely to different varieties of olive oil.

"Is there any point in going in?" said Maria. "It looks like a serious sort of place - we can't go in there with a tatty old photograph."

"We can. Look - it has air conditioning," Emma announced with the reverence usually reserved for religious experiences.

"It's not that hot," Rosie protested, though her sunhat was beginning to wilt in the midday sun.

"It's thirty-four degrees, you're wearing a hat, and I can see heat waves rising from the pavement," Emma replied. "We're going in."

"And what shall I say?"

"You'll think of something."

The cultural centre's interior was blissfully cool and unexpectedly charming. Whitewashed walls displayed local artwork, not the tourist-friendly seascapes they'd grown accustomed to, but real paintings that spoke of lives lived and stories told. An elderly woman at the reception desk looked up from her crossword puzzle and smiled.

"¿Puedo ayudarles?"

Maria fumbled for her phrase book, but before she could locate the relevant page, a voice from the back of the room called out in perfect English.

"Can I help you ladies?"

The voice belonged to a man emerging from behind a display case of ancient pottery. He was probably in his early sixties, like they were, with a weathered handsomeness that suggested a life spent outdoors and the slightly rumpled appearance of someone who cared more about books than ironing. His hair was silver at the temples, his shirt was the precise blue of Mediterranean sky, and when he smiled, Maria felt something stir in her chest that she'd forgotten was possible.

"We're looking for information about old buildings," she managed, grateful that her voice sounded steadier than she felt. "We have a photograph..."

"Ah, you're historians too?" His eyes lit up. "I'm Carlos Martinez, curator here. Please, let me see what you have."

Carlos, Maria repeated silently, filing the name away like a secret.

Emma and Rosie exchanged a look that Maria pretended not to notice as she extracted Lisa's photograph from her handbag. Carlos accepted it with the careful reverence of someone who understood that old photographs were more than just paper and chemicals - they were captured time & preserved dreams

Carlos studied Maria's face as she spoke about their quest - there was something about the way she balanced determination with vulnerability that made him want to help with more than just historical research. When she smiled, her whole face transformed, and he realised he was already hoping this wouldn't be a brief consultation.

His examination was thorough and professional. Maria

watched his hands as he held the photograph up to the light. They were good hands...strong, with long fingers and a thin white scar across the knuckles that spoke of some long-ago adventure. She wondered what story that scar told, then wondered why she was wondering.

"This is fascinating," Carlos murmured, his attention focused entirely on the image. "The architectural details... may I?" He gestured towards a magnifying glass on his desk.

"Of course," Maria said, then added impulsively, "It was our friend. She died recently, and we're trying to..." She paused, unsure how to explain their quest without sounding like three slightly unhinged women on a grief-fuelled mission.

"We're trying to find where she belonged," Emma finished quietly.

Carlos looked up from his examination, and the kindness in his eyes made Maria's chest tighten. "I'm sorry for your loss," he said simply. "Grief makes us do important things."

"Sometimes it makes us do ridiculous things," Rosie added, adjusting her sunhat. "We're still deciding which category this falls into."

Carlos laughed-a warm, genuine sound that filled the quiet space. "In my experience, the two categories overlap more than we'd like to admit." He returned his attention to the photograph. "But this isn't ridiculous at all. Look here-" He pointed to the tiles beneath Lisa's feet. "These are very specific. Hand-painted, traditional Majorcan style, but not the kind you find in tourist areas."

"These tiles were made by the Villa family, local artisans who worked primarily in the sixties and seventies. They supplied tiles for several institutions around the island." Carlos paused, studying the image more carefully. "The pattern, the colours... I believe these were used primarily for children's facilities."

The three women leaned forward simultaneously.

"Children's facilities?" Maria repeated.

"Schools, orphanages, children's homes. The Villa family had a contract with several charitable organisations." Carlos looked up, his expression thoughtful. "Your friend-was she from Majorca originally?"

"She was born in England and adopted as a baby," Rosie said. She came to England when she was very young. We never knew much about her early life."

"Well you're in luck. One of my specialities is adoption records from this period."

"Really?"

"Well, no, not really. Sorry. I was trying to be funny...very inappropriate. Huge apologies. I can try and help you, though. I know the place well and know lots of people. If you're serious about this search, I might be able to help."

"We're very serious," Maria said, then felt heat rise in her cheeks as she realised how that sounded. "About the search, I mean. Finding where this photograph was taken."

Carlos's smile was gentle and understanding. "I have contacts at the historical archives. With your permission, I could make some inquiries about children's homes that used Villa family tiles."

"That would be wonderful," Emma said. "Though we don't want to impose..."

"It would be my pleasure," Carlos assured them. "History is meant to be shared, not hoarded. Now, let me introduce you properly to Señora Rodriguez," Carlos said, gesturing towards the elderly woman at the reception desk who had been watching their interaction with obvious curiosity.

"Señora Rodriguez, a woman with silver hair pinned in an elegant chignon and a warm smile, immediately stood and moved towards them with arms outstretched, and leaned in for a kiss...the traditional Spanish greeting.

Maria, operating on decades of English conditioning, thrust out her right hand and stabbed the poor woman in the stomach, while Señora Rodriguez attempted to kiss her shoulder. Rosie then overcorrected and lunged forward so enthusiastically for the two-cheek kiss that she nearly headbutted the poor woman.

"Ay, Dios mío," Señora Rodriguez murmured."

I think we may have just invented a new form of international diplomacy," Rosie said, straightening her sunhat.

"Or started a very confusing dance," Emma added, stepping back with as much dignity as she could muster.

Carlos watched this cultural collision with barely suppressed laughter. "Perhaps we should practice," he suggested gently. "Left cheek first, then right. Just a light touch, no actual kissing required."

"Like air kissing, but more committed," Maria said, blushing to her roots as Carlos kissed her cheeks, then looked into her eyes.

"Now that we've mastered Spanish greetings, shall we discuss your photograph a little more with Señora Rodriguez? What was your friend's name?"

"Lisa," Maria said. "Her name was Lisa."

"Lisa," Carlos repeated the name as if testing how it felt. "She was a close friend?"

"She was," all three women said simultaneously, then laughed at their perfectly timed response.

"She was the sort of person who could make friends with a lamppost," Rosie added. "Always laughing, always doing something amazing."

"She would have loved this quest to find her story," Emma said softly.

Carlos nodded thoughtfully. "Then we must make sure her story has a proper ending."

He reached for a business card and a pen, his hand gently brushing Maria's as he handed over the card. Carlos held her gaze a moment longer than necessary. "I hope you find what you're looking for," he said, then added more quietly, "But even if you don't find the exact location, I suspect you'll discover something equally valuable. I'll help you all I can. May I reach you at your hotel?"

"We're staying at Villa Rosa Blanca," Maria said, then felt compelled to add, "It's... unique."

"Ah, you're staying at Señora Gutierrez's place." Carlos grinned. "She has very individual taste in decoration."

"That's one way to put it," Rosie said diplomatically.

"You haven't met Fernando yet, have you?" Carlos asked.

"Fernando?"

"The peacock. He has opinions about everything and isn't shy about sharing them. Usually around sunrise."

"Yep, we've met him," said Emma.

"I'll make a few calls, and I'll call you tomorrow evening, if that's acceptable?"

"Very acceptable," Maria managed, hoping she sounded more composed than she felt.

Carlos walked them to the door with the old-fashioned courtesy that was becoming endearingly familiar. "Ladies," he said, "I hope you find what you're looking for."

Outside in the blazing afternoon heat, the three women stood for a moment in contemplative silence.

"Well," Emma said finally. "That was illuminating."

"Very professional," Rosie agreed with elaborate innocence. "Such dedication to historical research."

"I have no idea what you're implying," Maria said with as much dignity as someone could muster while blushing furiously.

"We're not implying anything," Emma said serenely. "We're stating it outright. That man is completely smitten with you."

"Don't be ridiculous."

"Maria, darling," Rosie said gently, "when was the last time a man looked at you the way Carlos just did?"

Maria opened her mouth to protest, then closed it again. The truth was, she couldn't remember the last time anyone had looked at her with that kind of interested attention. Richard certainly hadn't in the last years of their marriage, and since the divorce, she'd convinced herself she was past the age where such things mattered. But standing in the Spanish sunshine, holding Carlos's business card like a small treasure, she realised she might have been wrong about quite a few things.

"He's going to help us find Lisa's door," she said finally.

"Oh, he's going to help with more than that," Rosie said with a wicked grin. "I can practically hear the wedding bells already."

"Rosie!"

"What? Life is short, Maria. Lisa would be the first person to tell you that."

"She would also tell you that some of the best adventures begin when you stop planning and start trusting," said Emma.

Maria looked down at the business card in her hand. *Carlos Martinez*, it read in elegant script. *Historian*. And below that, in smaller print: *Life is the art of drawing sufficient conclusions from insufficient premises.*

"Did you see this?" she asked, showing them the quote.

"Perfect," Rosie declared. "A philosopher and a historian. Lisa definitely would have approved."

As they walked back toward the bus stop, Maria smiled for reasons that had nothing to do with their quest and everything to do with the memory of kind eyes and gentle hands, and the possibility that some stories were just beginning.

LITTLE YELLOW CITROEN

Carlos arrived at Villa Rosa Blanca the next morning driving a car that looked like it had been designed by someone with a very optimistic view of what constituted road-worthy. The ancient Citroën was painted a cheerful yellow that had faded to the colour of old butter, and it rattled with the enthusiasm of maracas.

"Good Lord," Rosie said, peering through the villa's front window. "Is that thing held together with prayer and string?"

"Mostly prayer," Carlos called out cheerfully, seeing her through the open windows. "But she's been faithful for twenty years. We understand each other."

Maria emerged from the villa wearing a sundress she'd packed on impulse and never expected to wear—a soft blue that brought out her eyes and made her feel younger than she had in years. She'd told herself she was dressing for the warm weather, but the way Carlos's face lit up when he saw her suggested her subconscious might have had other ideas.

"Buenos días, ladies," he said, walking into their house and kissing each of them on both cheeks with the casual warmth that seemed to be standard Spanish greeting protocol. When he reached Maria, the kiss lingered just a fraction longer than strictly necessary, and she caught a hint of his cologne—something warm and woody that made her think of leather-bound books and quiet evenings by firelight.

"I hope you're ready for an adventure," he said, patting the Citroën's hood affectionately. "Esperanza here might not look like much, but she knows every road on this island."

"Esperanza?" Emma asked, settling into the car.

"Hope," Carlos translated. "My father named her. He said any car that ugly needed all the hope it could get."

Carlos adjusted the rearview mirror and pulled out a small notebook that had clearly seen better days.

"So, I made some calls this morning," he said, glancing back at his passengers. "Spoke to my cousin who works in construction, my friend at the historical society, even my old teacher who knows every building in the valley. If we're looking for blue ceramic tiles from the seventies, there are maybe four or five places worth checking."

Maria glanced at Carlos as he drove, noting how his hands moved expressively when he talked about island history. When he laughed at one of Rosie's jokes, the sound was warm and genuine, and she felt something flutter in her chest that had nothing to do with the winding mountain roads.

"You've been busy," Maria said, impressed by his thoroughness.

"It's not often I get to play detective. We'll start with the school in Sóller that used to be an orphanage. The orphanage has a reputation as one of the most compassionate on the island. Even locals who have never set foot inside it speak of it fondly.

"People said the nuns who ran it were known for their kindness, never turning away a child in need, and the teachers had a gift for making the children feel safe and wanted. It was the sort of place where birthdays were remembered, tears were wiped away without judgement, and no child ever felt forgotten."

"I love the sound of that," said Maria.

Carlos parked Esperanza under a plane tree that provided blessed shade, and they walked through gates decorated with cheerful murals of dancing children.

The headmistress, Señora Valdez, greeted Carlos like an old friend. She was a tiny woman with laughter lines that suggested a joyful, sun-filled life (and no interest in botox). She wore a floral dress colourful enough to hide playground mishaps and finger-painting dramas, and her handshake was firm enough to settle disputes between six-year-olds.

She welcomed the three women like honoured guests. She spoke English with the precision of someone who had been teaching it for decades.

"So you are the ladies on the mysterious quest," she said, leading them through corridors lined with children's artwork. "Carlos telephoned, very excited about historical tiles and a photograph you have. It sounds like your tiles are Villa family tiles. They are all over the island and very distinctive. See... here..."

She gestured to the floor, where Villa family tiles formed geometric patterns in blues and whites. They were beautiful, well-preserved, and.... absolutely nothing like the tiles in Lisa's photograph.

"Wrong pattern," Carlos said immediately. Disappointment emanated from the three women.

"Oh, I'm sorry," Señora Valdez said.

"These are from the Villa workshop, but a different commission entirely."

The children love these tiles. I'm sorry they can't help you with your quest."

"They are lovely. There's something almost musical about them," Maria said. "Like visual rhythms."

Carlos crouched beside Maria to examine the stonework. She was acutely aware of his proximity.

"Most people see tiles as decoration," he said to Senora Valdez. "We see them as clues."

She smiled warmly. "I wish you all the best, and if there's anything I can do to help, don't hesitate to ask."

Their second stop was a community centre that had once been an orphanage, perched on a hillside with views that stretched to the sea. The building was older, more weathered, with thick stone walls that spoke of decades of children's laughter and tears.

"This is more promising," Carlos said as they examined the entrance tiles. "Same period, same artisans, but look—"

He knelt beside the doorway, running his fingers along the edges of the ceramic work.

The tiles were indeed similar to those in Lisa's photograph—the same soft blues and whites, the same hand-painted quality. But the pattern was different, more elaborate, with small flowers scattered among the geometric designs.

"Close," Rosie said, crouching beside Carlos to examine the work. "But not quite right."

"The flowers are wrong," Maria agreed. "Lisa's tiles were simpler."

Carlos nodded thoughtfully. "There were several children's homes operating during that period. Some were privately funded, some run by religious orders, and some by the government. Each would have commissioned slightly different patterns."

As Carlos and the women looked down at the tiles in disappointment, the centre's director burst through the front doors like a whirlwind in sensible shoes—a woman in her forties with short-cropped hair and the kind of animated gesturing that suggested she'd had at least three cups of coffee already that morning.

"Carlos!" she called out, striding toward them with obvious

delight. "And these must be the mysterious English ladies hunting for blue doors. I'm Sophia."

Before anyone could respond, she had ushered them inside and was already putting a coffee pot on the stove.

"You want to know about our tiles, yes? Sit, sit—I have something that will interest you very much."

She disappeared into an office and returned moments later carrying a thick photo album that looked like it had survived several decades of enthusiastic handling. The cover was slightly warped, held together with what appeared to be Sellotape from the 1940s.

"This," Sophia announced with obvious pride, "is the complete visual history of our building. Every renovation, every celebration, every disaster—it's all here."

She spread the album open on the coffee table and began flipping through pages with the practised efficiency of someone who had given this tour many times before.

The early photographs were in black and white, formal compositions that spoke of institutional photography and special occasions.

"Here—1960s," Sophia said, pointing to a photograph of serious-faced nuns in traditional habits supervising a meal. The children sat in perfect rows at long wooden tables, their hands folded, their expressions suggesting that talking during dinner was not encouraged.

"Very different times then. Much more… structured."

She turned the page to reveal group photos from the 1970s —children arranged in neat rows for the camera, the older ones in back, the smaller ones sitting cross-legged in front. Everyone wore their best clothes, and several of the children had clearly been reminded to smile just before the photographer snapped the picture.

"And these are from Christmas celebrations," Sophia continued, her voice softening as she showed them photographs of holiday parties. The children wore paper crowns and held handmade decorations—construction paper angels, painted pinecones, stars cut from cardboard and covered with glitter that had probably taken weeks to clean up properly.

"Look at their faces," Emma said softly, studying a photo of children gathered around a Christmas tree that was clearly the product of much love and limited budget. "They look so hopeful."

"So many children passed through this place when it was an orphanage," Sophia said. "Most were adopted, some returned to families. We have records, but they're confidential, of course."

"Of course," Maria said, though her heart sank slightly.

"However," Sophia continued with a conspiratorial smile, "there is someone you should meet. Sister Soledad worked here for forty years. She's retired now, but she remembers every child who lived in this place. She has what you might call a photographic memory for faces."

"You're very kind," said Maria. "But we already know that this isn't the right place...the tiles are different."

"Ah, yes, but Sister Soledad will be able to remember whether your friend came here at any stage. Her memory for faces is extraordinary. I think you should talk to her. I think you'd find her to be useful to you in your search."

"Yes, that would be great, then. Could we meet her?" Emma asked.

"I'll telephone her this afternoon, and I'll call Carlos when I have news. "How about that?"

"We're so grateful. Thank you," they said, standing up and heading back towards the little yellow Citroen.

THE ALMOST-GIVING-UP

*T*he morning after their visit to the school and the community centre should have felt like progress. They had met wonderful people, heard promising stories, and been given the name of Sister Soledad, who supposedly knew every child who'd ever set foot in a children's home on the island.

But the villa felt oddly quiet when they returned. As if all the momentum had drained out of them.

Maria set the photograph of Lisa on the kitchen table and stepped back, studying it as though it might offer something new if she looked hard enough. Rosie poured coffee that none of them really wanted, and Emma drifted around the edge of the room, sketchbook in hand but no intention of drawing.

"Maybe," Emma said finally, her pencil tapping the page, "we've been chasing something that doesn't exist."

Maria turned, a little too quickly. "The photograph exists."

"But maybe that someone is gone," Rosie said, her voice gentle. "Maybe the place is gone. Maybe we're forty years too late."

No one spoke. The morning light slanted across the table,

touching the edges of their scattered notes—names, dates, scraps of half-remembered stories. Evidence in a case that refused to be solved.

Emma sank into a chair and rubbed her eyes. "I keep thinking about all the children in those photos. How many of them were adopted? How many were left there forever?"

Rosie closed her hand over Emma's. "You're doing that thing again," she said softly.

"What thing?"

"Taking everyone's sadness onto your own shoulders."

Emma tried to smile, but her chin wobbled. "I just... I don't want to get this wrong. I don't want to fail her."

Maria looked down at the photograph. Lisa, leaning against the blue door, smiling as if she knew something the rest of them didn't. That was the trouble with her—she always looked so certain, so invincible. Even in death.

"I miss her so much," Rosie said suddenly, her voice breaking. "I miss her laugh, and her terrible jokes, and the way she'd boss us all around and make it feel like an adventure instead of a nuisance."

"She would have found it," Maria whispered. "She would have charmed the information out of someone by now. Probably over two glasses of wine and a bowl of olives."

"She would have made it fun," Rosie said, tears streaking down her cheeks. "Even if we never found the door."

Maria reached for her hand across the table, and Emma slipped her own in to join them. For a while, they sat there like that—three women holding each other together in the quiet of an unfamiliar kitchen.

Eventually, Maria pulled in a shaky breath. "Maybe...maybe we should just pick somewhere beautiful and scatter her ashes there."

"The olive grove behind Carmela's farm was lovely," Emma offered, though her voice lacked conviction.

Rosie wiped her face with the heel of her hand. "I feel like we're letting her down."

"I feel like we're trying so hard to get it right," Maria said, her voice rough, "and still somehow failing."

Emma looked up, her eyes red. "Do you ever wonder what she'd say if she could see us now?"

They were quiet again, imagining Lisa standing at the head of the table, rolling her eyes at all this solemnity.

"She'd probably say, 'Oh for God's sake, stop crying and get a bottle of Rioja,'" Rosie said, a watery laugh escaping.

"She'd say, 'It doesn't matter where you put me, as long as you're together,'" Maria added.

"She'd say, 'And make sure you look fabulous doing it,'" Emma finished.

The laughter that bubbled up then was fragile and a little wild—an exhausted relief that they could still remember her voice clearly enough to hear it.

Maria leaned back, pressing her palms to her cheeks. "I don't know what we're supposed to do."

"I don't either," Rosie admitted.

Emma traced the edge of Lisa's photograph with her fingertip. "All I know is... I don't want to stop trying yet."

"Me neither," Maria said softly.

A breeze drifted through the open terrace doors, ruffling the papers. Maria reached out instinctively to catch the photograph before it slid to the floor. She held it in both hands, studying the details—the slight tilt of Lisa's head, the way her hair caught the light, the certainty in her smile.

Maybe that was the answer: not certainty, but showing up anyway. Keeping faith with the search, however long it took.

She looked up just as a figure appeared at the garden gate. Carlos stood there, a folder under his arm, watching them with an expression so kind it made something in her chest ache.

Rosie swiped at her cheeks, trying to compose herself. "We weren't expecting you," she called.

"I can see that," Carlos said, coming closer. "What's happened?"

They told him everything—how it felt as if they were chasing a story that didn't want to be found.

When Maria finished, she pressed the photograph to her chest, unable to look at him. "So you see," she said, her voice low, "we think it might be time to admit defeat rather than keep chasing. What if Sister Soledad doesn't know anything? What then? It's all so depressing to keep having disappointments."

Carlos glanced at each of them, then set his folder gently on the table.

"I've been asking people about Sister Soledad," he said. "She has a reputation for remembering every child she ever cared for. Every name, every face. If anyone can help you, it's her."

"Do you think she'll remember Lisa?" Emma whispered.

"I think," Carlos said gently, "she will remember something. And sometimes, one memory is all it takes."

For a long moment, none of them spoke. Then Rosie reached across the table and laid her hand over Maria's. "Maybe that's what Lisa would have wanted most of all," she said softly. "Not the perfect place, but the people who loved her refusing to give up."

Maria swallowed, her throat thick. "Tomorrow," she said, voice unsteady, "we find out who she was before she found us."

Rosie squeezed her hand. "And tonight...maybe we let ourselves be happy we've come this far."

Carlos looked at her then, and something passed between them—an understanding that sometimes, the best stories took their time unfolding.

And maybe, just maybe, they weren't finished yet.

THE FALSE TRAIL

$\mathcal{T}$he morning dawned grey and humid, with clouds hanging low over the mountains. Maria woke with a strange heaviness in her chest, as if the weather had seeped into her bones.

At breakfast, Emma spread out a new set of photographs she'd printed from her phone. "I've been thinking about the tiles," she said, tapping one image. "Look at this pattern. I found similar ones online last night."

Rosie leaned over, squinting. "Those do look almost identical."

"They're from a specific workshop in Santanyí," Emma continued, her voice gaining excitement. "The Forteza family. They only supplied tiles to five locations in the 1960s. I have the list."

Maria felt her pulse quicken. "Five locations? That's manageable."

"Better than that," Emma said. "Three are hotels that have since been demolished. One is a private home that's never had children. Which leaves..."

"Which leaves?" Rosie prompted.

"Casa dels Àngels. A children's sanctuary run by French nuns in the 1960s. It's about an hour from here."

The hope in the car was palpable as they wound through increasingly narrow mountain roads. Carlos drove while Maria navigated, her hands trembling slightly as she held the directions Emma had written out.

"The records I found said they specialised in taking children who were difficult to place," Emma explained from the back seat. "Children with health problems, behavioural issues, or just... those who had been passed over too many times."

"That could have been Lisa," Rosie said softly. "After losing her parents so young."

The building, when they finally found it, took their breath away. It sat perched on a hillside like something from a fairy tale – white walls, terracotta roof, and there, gleaming in the morning light, blue shutters and a blue door.

"Oh my God," Maria whispered.

They parked in silence, each woman caught in her own storm of emotion. The door was the right shade of blue. The building was the right size. Even the way the light fell seemed to match Lisa's photograph.

Carlos touched Maria's shoulder gently. "Shall we?"

The current owners were British...a couple who now ran it as a boutique hotel. They were welcoming but puzzled by the request to see historical records.

"We bought the place in 2001," the woman, Janet, explained. "It had been empty for years. We have some old photographs from the renovation, but nothing from when it was a children's home."

She led them to a small office where a collection of before-and-after photographs lined the walls. Maria's heart sank as she studied them. The tiles in the entryway were wrong – similar to Villa tiles, but not exact matches.

"Wait," Emma said suddenly. "Do you have any photos of the back entrance?"

Janet looked surprised. "The old service entrance? I think so..."

She pulled out another album, flipping through pages of construction photos. And there it was – a door, painted blue, with tiles that looked exactly like those in Lisa's photograph.

"That's it!" Rosie gasped. "That has to be it!"

But Carlos was frowning, studying the architectural details. "The stonework," he said slowly. "Look at the lintel. It's different."

"Stonework can be changed," Maria said, not wanting to let go of the hope.

"Yes, but..." Carlos pulled out his phone, comparing images. "The proportions are wrong. This doorway is narrower. And see here? The background in Lisa's photo shows part of a window. There's no window here."

The silence that followed felt like a physical weight.

"I'm so sorry," Janet said gently. "We do know the home kept records, though. They were transferred to the diocesan archives in Palma when the home closed. Perhaps..."

"Perhaps," Maria echoed, but the word felt hollow.

They drove back in defeated silence. The grey clouds had thickened, and by the time they reached the villa, rain was falling in sheets.

"I'll make tea," Emma said quietly once they were inside.

"I'll help," Rosie added, leaving Maria and Carlos alone in the sitting room.

Maria stood at the window, watching the rain streak the glass. "What if we never find it?" she asked, her voice barely audible. "What if we came all this way for nothing?"

Carlos moved to stand beside her. "Then you'll have honored your friend by trying. Isn't the search itself a form of love?"

"I wanted to find it for her," Maria said, tears threatening. "I

47

wanted to prove that her beginning mattered, that someone remembered."

"Someone does remember," Carlos said gently. "You do. And tomorrow, we'll keep looking."

That night, Maria lay awake listening to the rain against the tiles. She thought about Lisa – how she would have laughed at their earnest searching, how she would have turned even this disappointment into an adventure.

Don't give up on me now, Maria thought. *We're so close. I can feel it.*

SIGHTSEEING

The next morning, Carlos appeared at Villa Rosa Blanca earlier than expected, carrying a thermos of coffee and wearing the kind of smile that suggested he had plans beyond their usual research agenda.

"I have news," he said. "Sister Soledad can see us tomorrow at 4pm."

"Oh, that's great news," said Maria. "What should we do today? Are there any more leads we could follow?"

"I thought you might like to see Palma properly," he said, settling beside Maria on the terrace while Emma and Rosie were still getting ready. "Not the tourist version, but the real city. The one locals actually live in."

"That sounds wonderful," Maria said, though something in his voice made her study his face more carefully. "Is everything all right?"

Carlos hesitated, his fingers drumming against his coffee cup in a way that suggested nervousness. "I have a confession. Yesterday, when I was helping you research Lisa's story, I kept thinking about something else entirely."

"What were you thinking about?"

"About how much I wanted to show you my favourite places in the city. About how much I wanted to walk with you through streets that matter to me, to share pieces of my life that have nothing to do with historical research." He met her eyes directly. "I was thinking about how much I enjoy your company, and how that enjoyment has very little to do with your quest for Lisa's past. I'm sorry if I'm being inappropriate. I'm aware that I probably am."

Heat rose in Maria's cheeks that had nothing to do with the Spanish sun. "Carlos..."

"I'm not suggesting anything inappropriate," he said quickly. "I'm simply acknowledging that what I feel when I'm with you isn't entirely professional curiosity about your research project."

Before Maria could respond, Emma's voice carried from inside the villa: "Maria, are you ready to continue hunting for blue doors?"

"Actually," Carlos called back, "We're going to take a day off today - we're seeing Sister Soledad tomorrow, so we were going to resume our search after that. I'm planning to take Maria out for the day."

"Oooooo...," said Emma. "Right. Yes, great. That's a lovely idea."

She looked at the way Carlos and Maria were sitting, just slightly closer together than necessary, and grinned.

AN HOUR LATER, Maria and Carlos walked through Palma's old quarter, past buildings with centuries of layered history. He led her through narrow streets that tour groups never found, past shops where he was greeted by name, into courtyards where fountain music mixed with conversation in rapid Spanish.

"This is where I learned to love history," he said, stopping in a small plaza dominated by a church that looked medieval but felt alive with contemporary purpose. "Not in books, but in places like this, where you can feel how people have lived and loved and argued and celebrated for hundreds of years."

"It's beautiful," Maria said, watching elderly men play dominoes at café tables while children chased pigeons with the eternal optimism of the very young. "It feels... continuous. Like the past and present are having a conversation."

"Exactly." Carlos guided her to a bench beside the fountain, where they could observe the plaza's gentle theatre of daily life. "History isn't just what happened-it's what keeps happening. The patterns that repeat, the love that endures, the way people find ways to create meaning and beauty even in difficult circumstances."

"Is that why you do the adoption research?" Maria asked. "To help people find their patterns, their continuity?"

Carlos was quiet for a moment, watching a young mother negotiate with a toddler who had strong opinions about proper pigeon-chasing technique.

"Partly," he said finally. "But also because I understand what it feels like to live between stories. To know that part of your identity exists in a place you can't quite reach."

"What do you mean?"

"My father was Spanish, but my mother was Italian. I grew up hearing stories about relatives I'd never met, traditions I'd never experienced, a version of myself that existed only in my mother's memories." Carlos smiled, but there was something wistful in it. "She died when I was twenty, and suddenly half my history became inaccessible. I've spent my career helping other people bridge those gaps because I know how it feels to stand on one side of a story and wonder about the other side."

Maria studied Carlos with a new understanding. The passionate dedication to reuniting people with their histories wasn't just professional-it was deeply personal.

Maybe that's why she felt so comfortable with him. They

both knew what it was to start over, to rebuild a life brick by brick.

"Did you ever find your Italian family?" she asked gently.

"Some of them. Cousins, mostly. But the stories I really wanted-the ones about who my mother was before she became my mother-those were gone forever. I also wanted to find out more about my brother's past, but I'll save that story for another day."

He turned to face Maria directly. "This is why what you're doing for Lisa matters so much. You're preserving stories that would otherwise disappear. You're honouring not just her memory, but the people who helped shape her before you ever met her."

They sat in comfortable silence for a moment, watching the plaza's daily drama unfold around them. Maria felt something shifting between them-not the friendly collaboration of the past few days, but something deeper, more personal, more frightening in its implications.

"Carlos," she said carefully, "I need you to know that my life is complicated right now. I'm divorced, but only just, my children think I'm having some kind of breakdown by moving in with a group of women, and I have no idea what I'm going to do when this trip ends."

"I understand complicated," Carlos replied. "I'm fifty-eight years old, I've been married and divorced twice, I live alone with books and archaeological artefacts, and I just spent the morning rearranging my schedule so I could show an English woman my favourite plaza instead of cataloguing medieval pottery shards."

"That doesn't sound very sensible," Maria said, though she was smiling.

"Nothing about this feels sensible," Carlos agreed. "But it feels right. And I've learned that sensible and right aren't always the same thing."

Before Maria could respond, her phone buzzed with a text from her daughter Sarah: *Mum, what day are you back? You must have done it by now.*

The message felt like cold water thrown over the warm intimacy of the morning. Maria stared at the screen. Her daughter had grown up, for goodness's sake. Maria had done so much for them and carried them all for so long that they couldn't cope with her being away for any length of time. She tried to remember when she last went away...Gosh, years ago. She was entitled to this break, and she was entitled to say a fond farewell to Lisa.

"Everything all right?" Carlos asked, noticing her expression.

"My daughter," Maria said, holding up the phone. "She wants to know exactly when I'm coming home."

"And what do you think?"

Maria looked around the plaza, at the ancient stones and modern life, at Carlos, whose eyes held patience and possibility in equal measure, at the life she was discovering instead of the life she thought she was supposed to live. Oh, she knew that was silly; she hardly knew the man, but he made her feel great, and that was something she hadn't felt in ages.

"I think," she said slowly, "that I'm not ready to go home just yet."

Carlos's smile was like the sunrise. "Then shall we continue being unsuitably adventurous? I have at least six more favourite places to show you, and none of them appear in any guidebook."

They spent the rest of the morning wandering through Carlos's personal geography-the bookshop where he'd worked as a student, the restaurant where he'd had his first professional meeting as a curator, the hidden garden where he went when the weight of other people's lost histories became too heavy to carry alone.

With each stop, Maria felt herself falling a little deeper into something that was either wonderful or terrifying, and possibly both.

Carlos had the gift of making her feel interesting-not just as a tourist seeking help, but as a woman whose thoughts and reactions mattered, whose company was genuinely valued.

"There's one more place," he said as they approached the harbour, where fishing boats shared space with tourist vessels and the smell of salt water mixed with the aroma of grilled seafood from waterfront restaurants.

He led her to a small café perched on a pier, where tables overlooked water so blue it seemed artificial. The proprietor greeted Carlos with the enthusiasm reserved for family members, and within minutes, they were seated with coffee and pastries.

"This is where I come to think," Carlos said, watching seagulls perform aerial ballets over the harbour. "About work, about life, about whether I'm living the story I want to be living or just the one that seemed easiest at the time."

"And what conclusions do you usually reach?" Maria asked.

"That life is too short for stories that don't make you excited to wake up in the morning," Carlos replied. "That some risks are worth taking even when you can't predict the outcome. That some people are worth rearranging your entire understanding of what's possible."

The words hung between them like a bridge waiting to be crossed. Maria felt her heart hammering against her ribs with the kind of intensity she hadn't experienced since she was young enough to believe that anything was possible.

"Carlos," she began, but he reached across the table and covered her hand with his.

"You don't have to say anything now," he said gently. "I just wanted you to know where I stand. I wanted you to understand that what's happening between us isn't just vacation romance or helpful local assistance. It's something worth exploring, something that might be the beginning of a story neither of us planned but both of us need."

As they walked back through the city towards the car, Maria felt as though she were seeing Palma with completely different eyes. Not as a temporary stop on a quest to honour a dead friend, but as a place where people built lives that had nothing to do with duty or sensibility and everything to do with the possibility that love could find you at any age, in any circumstances, when you were finally brave enough to recognise it.

She realised she wasn't ready for the day to end. Every winding street they'd explored with Carlos had peeled back another layer of the city's quiet magic, and something in her felt almost weightless with the possibility of it all.

They paused at a little square where the lanterns were just starting to flicker on. Carlos turned to her, smiling.

"Shall we call it a day?" he asked, though his tone suggested he hoped she'd say no.

Maria looked out over the rooftops, feeling a softness she couldn't quite name. "Not yet. But I should check on the others. Rosie and Emma will be wondering if I've been kidnapped."

"Then let's collect them," he said easily. "There's a place I think you'd all like. Not touristy. A friend of mine owns it."

"A friend?"

"He's—" Carlos hesitated, as though weighing how to describe Miguel. "Let's say he's someone who knows everyone on this island and has never once cooked a bad meal."

Maria felt herself smile, warmed by the thought that this evening might be about more than just the next clue in Lisa's story.

"All right," she said. "Let's go back and fetch the others."

They drove through streets that were just beginning to wake for the night—waiters lighting candles on terraces, couples strolling arm in arm—and by the time they reached Villa Rosa

Blanca, Rosie and Emma were already out on the porch with glasses of wine in hand.

"There you are!" Rosie called. "We thought you'd eloped."

"Not yet," Maria teased. "But Carlos has promised us dinner somewhere special."

Emma brightened. "I vote yes to dinner."

"Good," Carlos said. "Then it's settled. Shall we?"

Together, the four of them climbed into the little yellow Citroën, the night ahead stretching out like a promise none of them quite dared to name.

THE PLACE CARLOS had in mind turned out to be a tapas bar tucked into a narrow street in Valldemossa. *Casa Flamenca* was the kind of establishment that existed more by reputation than signage—you either knew it was there, or you didn't deserve to find it.

"This doesn't look like much," Rosie observed, studying the understated wooden door that bore no identifying marks except for the faint sound of music seeping through the ancient wood.

"The best places never do," Carlos replied, pressing a buzzer Maria hadn't noticed. "Some experiences require a leap of faith."

The door opened to reveal a man who looked like he had stepped out of a Hemingway novel—weathered face, knowing eyes, and the kind of casual elegance that made you feel immediately under-dressed.

"Carlos," he said warmly, embracing their guide with genuine affection. "You bring us visitors on a Wednesday night? This must be special."

"Very special, Miguel. These ladies are on a quest for answers about a friend's past."

"Ah, quests for the past," Miguel's eyes twinkled as he gestured them inside. "Those are the most important kind.

Welcome to my humble establishment. I am Miguel Herrera, and this place has been collecting stories for forty years."

The interior was a revelation. Stone arches supported a vaulted ceiling from which lanterns hung, casting swaying shadows on walls lined with guitars and photographs.

"Every corner of this room has stories," Miguel explained, leading them to a table in front of a small stage. "Stories about the people who built it, the people who danced here, the people who came to forget, and the people who came to remember."

Rosie ran her fingers along a wall covered with framed black-and-white photographs. "It feels like the kind of place where time stops."

"Or loops back on itself," Maria added quietly.

Miguel gave her a thoughtful look, as if he could see right through her to the reason they were there. "Some places do that," he said. "They hold memory like a song waiting to be played again."

He disappeared behind the bar, returning with glasses of rich red wine and a plate of olives glistening with oil.

"On the house," he said, placing everything in front of them. "For pilgrims."

"Thank you," Emma said softly.

Miguel inclined his head. "If you need anything—directions, names, stories—just ask. I've been here long enough to know a little about everything."

As they settled at their table, Rosie found her gaze drawn to Miguel again and again. It wasn't just that he was handsome—though he was, in that understated, quietly confident way that had always appealed to her more than any polished charmer. It was something about how he carried himself, how he seemed entirely at ease in his own skin.

She tried to focus on the conversation, but her mind kept drifting. She was surprised by how natural it felt to notice someone, to feel that gentle spark of curiosity flickering to life again after so long. Every time she looked up, Miguel seemed to be watching her too, his eyes warm, assessing. When he smiled —just a small, private curve of his mouth—it did something to her chest she wasn't sure she was ready for.

A little while later, she slipped away to find the bathroom, needing a moment to collect herself. But when she emerged, she nearly collided with him in the narrow corridor. For a heartbeat, neither of them moved.

"Forgive me," he said softly, though his expression suggested he wasn't sorry at all. His eyes flicked to her mouth before returning to hers, and the heat of it startled something awake inside her.

"It's fine," she managed, her voice a little huskier than she liked.

He gestured toward the bar. "Can I tempt you to a drink before you rejoin your friends?"

She hesitated—just long enough to feel that sweet, unfamiliar thrum of anticipation—and then nodded. "Why not?"

When Emma and Maria eventually looked over, Rosie was perched on a barstool, leaning in close as Miguel spoke to her in that quiet, attentive way that made it feel like she was the only person in the room. She laughed at something he said and brushed her hair back from her face, and for the first time in what felt like forever, she wasn't thinking about before or after —only about this moment, and how good it felt to be noticed again.

At the table, Maria lifted her glass and tilted her head toward the bar. "Look at her. She looks happy."

"She does," Emma agreed softly. "It's lovely to see."

Carlos smiled. "Well, now we need to find someone equally charming for you, Emma, so you three can stay in Spain forever."

"Don't tempt us," Maria said, laughing. "I could get used to this."

"Just imagine," Carlos teased. "One romance for each of you. A proper Majorcan adventure."

Later, as they were leaving, Miguel walked them to the door. He held Rosie's gaze a moment longer than necessary, then slipped a folded piece of paper into her hand.

"In case you get lost," he said. His smile was unmistakable—gentle, but with the promise of something more if she wanted it.

Her heart gave a little kick, almost giddy. She tucked the paper into her bag, feeling the tiniest tremor in her fingers, and told herself she was being ridiculous. But as they stepped out into the warm night, she already knew she'd look at that number before she went to sleep. Just to be sure it was real.

MEETING SISTER SOLEDAD

*M*aria woke up with a strange mixture of excitement and apprehension. They were so close now. But what if Sister Soledad didn't remember Lisa? What if this was just another beautiful dead end?

Carlos could sense that she was worrying when he came to collect the women.

"You're worrying," Carlos observed as he opened the car door for her.

"I'm always worrying," Maria admitted. "It's one of my less attractive qualities."

"I disagree," he said quietly. "Your worry comes from love. That's always attractive."

Maria noticed Rosie and Emma nudging one another and smiling.

SISTER SOLEDAD WAS unlike anyone they had expected to meet. When the current administrator had mentioned that one of the original nuns still lived in the village, they had imagined a frail, confused elderly woman who might peer at them through thick glasses and offer them dusty biscuits while vaguely remembering fragments of the past.

Instead, they found themselves facing a woman who was ninety-two years old but possessed eyes like black pearls that missed absolutely nothing, and a mind that could have put a computer to shame-the type of computer that never crashed, never forgot where it saved files, and definitely never needed to ask "Have you tried turning it off and on again?"

"You look surprised," Sister Soledad said with obvious amusement, catching their expressions. "Were you expecting someone more... decrepit?"

"We weren't expecting someone who looked like she could still run a marathon," Rosie admitted.

"Only half marathons these days," Sister Soledad replied with a perfectly straight face. "I have to pace myself."

She invited them into her small flat with an old-world courtesy that made refusing impossible, settling them around a table laden with photographs, documents, and what appeared to be sixty years' worth of carefully preserved memories. The walls were covered with pictures of children-graduation photos, wedding announcements, baby pictures sent by former residents who still considered her family.

"You have questions about our children," she said in careful English, her accent thick but her meaning crystal clear. "I remember them all. Every face, every story, every heartbreak and every joy."

Maria placed Lisa's photograph on the table with trembling hands, hardly daring to hope after so many disappointments. "We're trying to find out about this woman. We think she might have been here in the 1960s, but we're not certain...obviously, this picture was taken years later, but we're wondering whether you recognise her at all?"

Sister Soledad looked at the picture and smiled. "I know who that is. I know very well. It is little Lisa. Oh, I haven't seen her as a grown-up. How lovely she became."

The women stood in silence while Carlos showed the pictures of the tiles.

"Ah, sí. Those are Villa family tiles-they supplied many places in the 1960s. But this blue door..." She tapped Lisa's photograph. "This is not from our facility. Our doors were always brown wood, very plain."

"Then where?" Maria asked.

"Lisa talked about 'la casa azul,' the blue house. It was where she stayed for maybe five years before coming to us. A foster family, very kind people. She said it was the first place after her parents died where she felt safe."

"So the photograph was taken at this foster home?" Emma asked.

"I believe so," Sister Soledad nodded. "Lisa would draw pictures of it sometimes...always the same blue door, always tiles like these. The Villa family supplied tiles to foster homes that worked with the Catholic charities. It created continuity for children who moved between places."

Sister Soledad adjusted the small reading glasses that hung from a chain around her neck and took Lisa's photograph in her weathered hands again. "Now, let me look at this face properly..."

For a long moment, she studied the image in complete silence, her expression unreadable. The three friends held their breath, waiting.

Then her face transformed. The careful politeness melted away, replaced by a smile that carried decades of love, loss, and treasured memories. Her eyes filled with tears that she didn't bother to wipe away.

"Ah, sí," she whispered, her voice thick with emotion. "Little Lisa."

Sister Soledad's weathered fingers traced Lisa's young face in the photograph with infinite tenderness, as if she were greeting an old friend. "Such a dancer, that one. Always spinning, always laughing. She would make crowns from the olive leaves and declare herself Queen of the Mountains."

Maria felt the world shift slightly on its axis.

"Lisa Rosario," Sister Soledad said, her voice growing stronger as memories flooded back. "She came to us when she was perhaps six years old. So thin at first. But ah, what spirit she had once she began to trust us. She would dance for the other children, make up little songs, organise elaborate games of make-believe."

"Lisa," Rosie whispered, staring at the photograph.

"We had no idea," Maria said, her voice barely audible. "She never said anything about... about any of this."

Sister Soledad nodded knowingly. "Many of our children chose not to speak of their early years. The pain, you understand. Some wounds go very deep, even when they heal."

"But why would she keep this photograph?" Emma asked, trying to piece together a puzzle they hadn't even known existed. "Why hold onto this memory if it was painful?"

Sister Soledad set the photograph down carefully and looked at each of them in turn. "Because it was not all painful, I think. Lisa was with us for four or five years before the English family came for her. But in that time, and at her foster home, she found her joy. She learned to laugh, to trust, to hope."

"She was adopted by an English family?" Maria asked.

"Sí. A lovely couple who could not have children of their own. They saw Lisa during one of their visits and..." Sister Soledad smiled. "It was love at first sight, as you say. They gave her a new life in England. But she never forgot us. She wrote letters for many years, sent photographs."

Sister Soledad stood and moved to a tall wooden cabinet, its doors carved with religious scenes. She withdrew a small wooden box, the kind used to store precious things. Inside were letters, postcards, and photographs-decades of correspondence.

"Here," she said, spreading some of the items on the table. "Letters from Lisa in England. Always she wrote about her new life, her school, and her friends. But always she asked about the children here, about the sisters, about home."

Maria picked up one of the letters, written in Lisa's familiar handwriting but dated nearly forty years ago. The paper was thin, the ink slightly faded, but the words were unmistakably their friend's voice-warm, funny, full of life and curiosity about the world.

"'Dear Sister Soledad,'" Maria read aloud, "'I hope this letter finds you well and that the new children are settling in nicely. I think of you often, and of my foster family, especially when I see blue doors or ceramic tiles. They always remind me of being safe...'"

Her voice caught on the last word.

"Safe," Emma repeated softly. "She felt safe."

"The foster family with the blue door helped, but they could only keep her for a short while. When she came to us, she would wake crying in the night, asking for her mama and papa. But slowly, slowly, she began to heal."

She selected another photograph from her collection-a group shot of children and nuns taken in what appeared to be the 1960s. There, in the front row, was a little girl with dark hair and familiar eyes, grinning at the camera with a pure joy that only children possess.

"There she is," Sister Soledad said proudly. "My little dancer."

The three friends stared at the photograph, seeing their sophisticated, elegant Lisa as a small, orphaned child who had somehow found the strength to smile again.

"She looks so happy," Rosie said, her voice thick with emotion.

"She was happy, by the end," Sister Soledad confirmed. "That is what made letting her go so difficult, but also so joyful. We knew she was ready for a family, ready to love and be loved again."

"But why didn't she ever tell us about any of this?" Maria asked the question that had been haunting her since Sister Soledad's first recognition.

Sister Soledad considered this carefully. "Perhaps because her life with you began when her healing was complete. Perhaps she wanted to be only the Lisa you knew-successful, confident, full of light. The frightened child, the grieving orphan-perhaps she felt those parts of her story were finished."

"But they weren't finished," Emma said quietly. "They were part of who she was."

"Sí, but not parts she needed to carry into her future. Some people must leave their past behind to move forward. Others must embrace it. Lisa chose to leave hers here, with us, where it could be safe."

Sister Soledad returned to her box of memories and withdrew one more item-a small, hand-painted ceramic tile, blue and white, with a simple flower pattern.

"She made this for me during her last week here," Sister Soledad said, placing it gently on the table. "She wanted to paint something that would stay even after she left. 'For remembering,' she told me."

Maria touched the tile with reverent fingers. Lisa's work, created by her small hands decades before they'd ever met. The tile was slightly lopsided, the flower charmingly imperfect in the way of children's art, but it radiated love and hope and the determination to create beauty even in difficult circumstances.

"She kept creating," Emma said wonderfully. "Even as a child, she was an artist."

"Always," Sister Soledad agreed. "She would draw on any scrap of paper, paint with mud if we had no proper paints, tell stories that made the other children laugh until their bellies hurt. Art was how she processed the world, how she made sense of loss and love."

"That never changed," Rosie said softly. "She was still doing that when she died. Still creating, still making people laugh, still turning pain into something beautiful."

They sat in comfortable silence for a moment, absorbing the weight of revelation and the strange comfort of finally understanding their friend's mysterious past.

"The photograph," Maria said finally, holding up Lisa's image. "Why do you think she kept this particular one?"

Sister Soledad smiled. "Because it shows her at the blue door. The place where she first felt safe again after losing her parents. It was her reminder that even after the worst things happen, it is possible to find safety, to find home again."

"'Where my true story began,'" Emma quoted from the back of the photograph. "She didn't mean it was the beginning of her life. She meant it was the beginning of her healing."

"Of her hope," Maria added.

"Of learning that she could be loved again," Rosie finished.

Sister Soledad nodded approvingly. "You understand her well, even without knowing this part of her story. That is the mark of true friendship."

As they prepared to leave, Sister Soledad made them promise to stay in touch, to send photographs from England, and to remember that they would always have family in Spain. She gave them copies of some of Lisa's letters and the address of the foster family who had cared for her before the children's home.

"The Mendoza family," she said. "They are very old now, but they might remember Lisa. They live in Valldemossa house with the blue door that your friend painted so many times."

"The actual blue door from the photograph?" Emma asked.

"I believe so. Lisa used to say she could never forget that door because it was the first one that opened to kindness."

"And do you know the address?"

"NO, I'm afraid I don't, but Carmen will. She runs a community centre now in what used to be another children's facility, up in the mountains near Santa Eulalia. Carmen worked there in the 1970s when it was still caring for children. She knows many stories about the different places children lived during that time, and she has an excellent memory for faces."

Sister Soledad disappeared momentarily and returned with a small piece of paper bearing an address written in careful script.

"Carmen might recognise your photograph," she continued. "But first…" Her eyes twinkled with the kind of mischief that suggested she was about to propose something wonderful. "Carmen's daughter is getting married tomorrow in Santa Eulalia. She invited me, and I know she would welcome Lisa's friends. Spanish weddings are celebrations of life and love— exactly what Lisa would want for you."

"We couldn't possibly gate-crash a wedding," Maria protested, though something in her voice suggested she was already imagining the possibility.

Sister Soledad looked at Carlos and shrugged her shoulders as if confused. "Gate-crash?"

"Gate-crash means to force entry when you are not welcome," he explained.

"Ah. Such a funny expression. In Spain, there is no such thing as gate-crashing a wedding," Sister Soledad said with obvious delight. "There is only joining a celebration of love. Besides, Carmen will be there, and what better way to meet someone than at their daughter's happiest moment?"

As they walked back to Carlos's car, clutching their friend's childhood drawings and Sister Soledad's directions to Santa Eulalia, Maria realised that their quest was taking on a life of its own—each discovery leading not just to more information, but to more connections, more stories, more reasons to believe that some journeys were guided by forces bigger than logic.

. . .

LATER THAT EVENING, when the others were content to sit on the terrace with a bottle of wine, Rosie found herself glancing at her phone more than once, wondering if she dared.

Eventually, she slipped away to the little path at the end of the garden, her heart tripping in her chest. Miguel had sent a simple message earlier—*Come walk with me if you feel like it*—and she'd been unable to think about anything else since.

Miguel was waiting by the old stone wall overlooking the sea, his hands tucked into his pockets, one foot resting casually against the mossy stones. He straightened as she approached, and the way his face softened made her feel oddly lightheaded.

"I wasn't sure you'd come," he said.

She smiled, feeling her pulse flutter. "I wasn't sure either."

They began to walk, the hush of evening settling around them like a secret. Now and then, their shoulders brushed, and each time, a little shiver of anticipation rippled through her.

They paused at a curve in the lane where wild rosemary spilled over the wall, fragrant and untamed. Miguel plucked a sprig and held it out.

"For your pocket," he said. "So you'll remember this walk."

She took it, unable to stop the smile that spread across her face. "I think I will anyway."

They strolled on, their steps falling into an easy rhythm. Rosie felt the warmth of his palm brush against the back of her hand, and before she could think herself out of it, she turned her hand over to link her fingers with his.

He looked down at their joined hands, then back at her with a slow, careful smile. "That's better," he murmured.

When they reached the little square, she stopped and turned to face him. For a heartbeat, neither of them spoke.

"I like this," she said quietly. "I like...you."

His thumb skimmed over her knuckles, the gentlest touch. "Then let's see where it goes."

He leaned in and kissed her, slow and warm, tasting of red wine and salt air. When they drew apart, her heart was beating so fast she had to laugh.

"I should go before I disgrace myself," she whispered.

"I'll walk you back," he said, and this time she didn't pretend to protest.

When she slipped back through the villa door, Emma and Maria were pretending not to look up. Rosie pressed a hand to her flushed cheek and let herself smile, feeling more alive than she had in years.

THE GATE CRASHERS

*T*he morning sun streaming through Villa Rosa Blanca's windows revealed three women in various states of wardrobe crisis.

"I can't wear this to a Spanish wedding," Emma declared, holding up a sensible beige dress. "I look like I'm going to a library conference. Why did I bring this?"

"You look like you're going to run a library conference," Rosie corrected, emerging from her room in a flowing red dress that made her look as though she was planning to dance until dawn. "Which is exactly why you're not wearing it. Let's have a look at what else you've got. We'll have to buy you something if everything in that bag is as dull as that dress."

Maria appeared in the doorway wearing a brown and gold sundress that brought out her eyes and made her look younger than she had in years. The transformation didn't go unnoticed.

"Well, well," Rosie said with obvious delight. "Someone's making an effort for a certain Spanish historian."

"It's just a dress," Maria protested, though her cheeks were already pink.

"It's just a dress that you've never worn before and happens to be exactly the colour of Carlos's eyes," Emma observed.

"I have no idea what colour Carlos's eyes are," Maria said with the dignity of someone who absolutely knew they were dark brown with flecks of gold around the edges.

"Of course you don't, darling. Just like you had no idea you were humming Spanish love songs while you made coffee this morning."

"Those weren't love songs. They were just... songs. That happened to be Spanish."

"Songs that Carlos taught you yesterday," Emma added helpfully.

"Songs that you specifically asked him to teach you," Rosie continued, "because you wanted to 'understand Spanish culture better.'"

Maria looked at her reflection in the hallway mirror and realised that her friends were absolutely right. She was making an effort, and not just for the wedding. She was making an effort for Carlos, for the possibility of dancing with him again, for the growing certainty that whatever was happening between them was worth the risk of looking foolish.

"Fine," she said, smoothing her dress with hands that were only slightly trembling. "I like him. I like him rather a lot, actually. Are you satisfied?"

"Delighted," Rosie said, kissing her cheek. "Lisa would be so proud."

An hour later, they were winding through mountain roads toward Santa Eulalia, a village perched on the mountainside like a collection of sugar cubes someone had scattered and forgotten to collect. White houses with terracotta roofs clustered around a church whose bell tower had been chiming the hour with stubborn regularity since approximately the Middle Ages, and narrow streets wound between buildings that seemed to have grown from the rock itself.

"It's like a fairy tale," Emma said as Carlos navigated Esperanza through streets barely wide enough for a donkey, let alone a car.

"A fairy tale where everyone's invited to a party, apparently," Rosie observed, pointing to the festive decorations that draped every balcony and doorway.

Ribbons in white and gold fluttered from windows, flowers spilled from every available container, and the sound of music and laughter echoed off the ancient stone walls.

"Sister Soledad was right about Spanish weddings being celebrations of life," Maria noted, watching children in their finest clothes chasing each other between the decorated doorways.

"Saturday weddings," Carlos explained, parking the car in a square dominated by a fountain that had been decorated with enough flowers to stock a florist's shop. "In villages like this, the whole community celebrates."

They climbed out of the car, legs grateful for the stretch after the winding mountain drive. The former religious complex was housed in what had clearly once been a substantial monastery—buildings arranged around a central courtyard with the kind of weathered stone architecture that spoke of centuries and serious purpose.

"There," Emma said, pointing to a blue door set into an arched entranceway. "That could be it. The stonework looks right—it matches the background in Lisa's photograph."

The door was the right shade of blue, and the stonework did indeed match the background of Lisa's photograph. But as they approached, it became clear that today was not going to be a day for quiet investigation.

The courtyard beyond the blue door was filled with people in their finest clothes, and the air thrummed with the distinctive energy of a celebration in full swing.

"This is going to be wonderful," Emma said, already

sketching the scene—women in elegant dresses chatting in animated groups, children in miniature formalwear chasing each other between the adults, elderly men in serious discussion about topics that were clearly of vital importance.

"I do love a good party," Rosie said with satisfaction. "And Sister Soledad was right—this is exactly what Lisa would have wanted for us."

Before they could take in much more of the scene, a woman in a dress that was more flowers than fabric approached them with the kind of smile that suggested they were exactly who she'd been hoping to see.

"¡Bienvenidas!" she called out, gesturing enthusiastically. "You must be Sister Soledad's friends! I am Carmen, and this—" she gestured toward the festivities with obvious pride, "—is my daughter's wedding day."

"Your daughter's wedding," Maria said warmly. "Thank you so much for welcoming us. Sister Soledad spoke of you with such affection."

"Soledad is like family to us," Carmen replied, linking arms with Maria and Rosie with the kind of maternal authority that brooked no argument. "Come, you must have champagne and meet everyone. Everyone is so curious about the English ladies with the mysterious photograph."

Emma found herself swept along in their wake, marvelling at how they'd gone from historical investigation to honoured wedding guests in the space of thirty seconds.

The courtyard was even more magical up close—ancient stone walls draped with fairy lights, long tables covered in white linens and laden with food that made her mouth water just looking at it, and a small band tuning their instruments in preparation for what promised to be an evening of serious celebration.

"The bride is beautiful," Emma said, nodding toward a young woman in a dress that managed to be both traditional and modern, surrounded by a cloud of friends and relatives who were having the time of their lives.

"She is perfect," Carmen agreed with the satisfaction of a mother whose daughter had chosen well. "And her new husband, he is a good boy. Owns a restaurant in Palma, makes excellent paella."

Emma caught Rosie's eye, and they shared a moment of silent communion, both thinking the same thing—this was going to be much better than their usual English fare.

"Now," Carmen continued, "you must show me this famous photograph. Sister Soledad told me about your quest, and everyone is curious."

Word had apparently spread through the wedding party like wildfire, because within minutes Maria found herself surrounded by interested faces as she produced Lisa's picture.

The photograph was passed from hand to hand with the reverence usually reserved for religious artifacts, each person studying it with the serious attention of expert witnesses.

"The door, yes, that is our door," confirmed an elderly man whose formal suit couldn't quite conceal the paint stains on his fingers. "But this photograph, it is from before. When this place was for children, not for artists."

"You remember when it was a foster home?" Maria asked hopefully.

"Oh yes. I remember."

A woman in her sixties, clearly related to Carmen by the family resemblance and the shared talent for dramatic gestures, leaned over to study the photograph more closely.

"This girl," she said, pointing to Lisa's young face. "She looks familiar. But not from here, I think. From the artists retreat in Valldemossa. It used to be a foster home."

"That's what I just said. Are you deaf?" said the old man.

"Valldemossa," Rosie repeated thoughtfully. "That's where Miguel has his restaurant."

"Yes, that's right."

"Do you have an address, or number, or can you tell us where this house is? We want to scatter our friends ashes there."

"MY cousin will come with the number. She is not here yet but she has the information. She will find you."

Before Maria could pursue this promising lead, the band struck up a traditional wedding march, and the crowd began organising themselves for what was clearly an important moment in the proceedings.

Carmen grabbed Maria's arm. "The bouquet throwing!" she announced. "All the ladies must participate. For luck!"

"Oh, we couldn't possibly—" Maria began, but she was already being propelled toward a group of women ranging in age from teenagers to grandmothers, all positioned strategically in front of a slightly elevated platform where the bride stood, bouquet in hand.

"I'm sixty-four years old," Rosie protested, though she was laughing. "Surely there's an age limit on bouquet catching."

"Love has no age limit," declared a woman who had to be eighty if she was a day, elbowing her way to the front of the group with the determination of a rugby player.

Emma found herself caught up in the excitement despite her natural inclination toward observing rather than participating.

The bride, radiant with happiness and perhaps a glass or two of champagne, was clearly enjoying the anticipation she was building as she prepared to launch the bouquet.

"¡Tres, dos, uno!" the crowd chanted, and the bouquet sailed through the air in a perfect arc.

Time seemed to slow as Maria watched the flowers tumble through the sunshine, white roses and baby's breath rotating lazily against the blue sky. She had a moment to think that it was heading nowhere near her, that she was safe from whatever embarrassment might come from catching a wedding bouquet at her age, and then—

The bouquet landed squarely in Rosie's outstretched hands.

The cheer that went up from the wedding guests could probably have been heard in the next village.

As the music wound down and the last of the confetti settled into the grass, Maria found herself standing near the buffet, absently watching the newlyweds pose for photographs.

A woman in a pale green dress approached, her hands clasped in front of her. She looked familiar—one of the cousins, perhaps, or a neighbour.

"You are the English ladies searching for the blue door?" she asked, her voice soft but certain.

Maria blinked, startled. "Yes—yes, we are."

The woman nodded thoughtfully. "Carmen suggested I tell you about the house with the blue door."

"Do you know where the house is?"

"I do." She reached into her handbag and withdrew a folded scrap of paper. "It has changed hands many times, but the blue door is still there."

Maria took the paper with trembling fingers. A single address, neatly printed. A phone number, carefully written.

"Thank you," she whispered.

"Some stories want to be found," the woman said simply. "I hope you find yours."

LADIES WHO LUNCH

The next morning, the address sat on the kitchen table like a living thing, radiating possibility and dread in equal measure.

Rosie held her phone in both hands, staring at the screen as though it might explode. "Someone else should do it," she muttered.

Maria reached for the phone, then pulled her hand back. "I can't. My Spanish isn't good enough, and I'll start crying."

Emma let out a nervous laugh. "Fine. I'll do it. My Spanish is non-existence, but I have balls of steel" She took a steadying breath and dialled the number, pressing the speaker button so they could all hear.

A woman answered, her voice warm but cautious. As Emma explained why they were calling, Maria and Rosie gripped each other's hands under the table.

"Yes," the woman said when Emma finished. "I know the house you mean. My parents have lived there since 1987. You are welcome to come."

Emma swallowed. "When would be convenient?"

"Tomorrow morning. We'll expect you at ten."

When the call ended, nobody moved. Relief, fear, and something like reverence filled the quiet.

Rosie exhaled shakily. "Well. That's that."

Maria nodded. "Today, we sightsee."

Emma lifted her chin. "Today, we remember we're still alive."

And for the first time in days, they all managed to smile.

CARLOS SUGGESTED they have lunch in Palma, somewhere shaded and quiet after the morning's call.

Rosie waited until Carlos pulled the little yellow Citroën to a stop outside the restaurant before she cleared her throat. "I should probably mention," she began, her voice a little too bright, "that I've…well…I've invited Miguel to join us for lunch."

Maria turned in her seat, eyebrows arched. "Miguel?"

Rosie felt her cheeks grow warm. "We've seen each other a couple of times. Nothing dramatic. Just…walks, a coffee here and there." She glanced down at her hands and then back up, unable to stop the small smile that crept across her face. "I like him. He's…easy to be around."

When they walked into the little square, Rosie spotted Miguel immediately. He was leaning against the sun-warmed wall, sleeves rolled to his elbows, studying the menu board as though he had all the time in the world.

She felt something flutter low in her belly, absurd and wonderful.

"Fancy seeing you here," she called, trying to sound casual.

He looked up, his face brightening in a way that made warmth bloom behind her ribs. "I was hoping you'd come."

Maria exchanged a look with Emma and tried not to smile too broadly.

The interior of the restaurant was exactly what Maria had

secretly hoped for—crowded, noisy, filled with animated conversation that suggested people came here as much for the company as the food. Carlos was greeted like family, kissed on both cheeks by a woman who could have been anywhere from sixty to eighty and clearly ran the place through sheer force of personality.

"Señora Gutierrez," Carlos said, "I'd like you to meet my friends from England."

What followed was a rapid exchange in Spanish that involved much gesturing, several glances at the three women, and what sounded like maternal interrogation.

"What is she saying?" Emma whispered.

"She's asking if you're married, if you have children, and why such beautiful women are travelling without husbands," Carlos translated, trying to keep a straight face. "Also, she wants to know if you can cook."

"What did you tell her?" Rosie asked.

"That you're independent, accomplished, and perfectly capable of taking care of yourselves." He hesitated, then added, "And that Maria is learning Spanish and would appreciate patient conversation practice."

Maria groaned, but Señora Gutierrez beamed and seized her hand in both of hers, launching into an enthusiastic lesson that made no allowance for beginner nerves.

While Maria practised her halting Spanish under Señora Gutierrez's watchful eye, Rosie and Miguel slipped easily into conversation.

"So," he murmured, leaning in, "tell me something you haven't told anyone else this week."

She toyed with her napkin, trying to look composed. "I… miss this. The feeling that anything could happen."

His thumb brushed lightly over her knuckles. "Then let's make sure something does."

Across the table, Emma sighed theatrically. "This is so unfair. Maria's got Carlos, Rosie's got Miguel. Who exactly am I supposed to flirt with?"

"You have Señora Gutierrez," Rosie teased. "She seems very fond of you."

Emma widened her eyes in mock horror. "All I want from this trip is to scatter the ashes and rediscover my art. That's all I want."

Maria smiled. "And eat all the tapas Majorca can provide."

"That too," Emma admitted.

Señora Gutierrez paused long enough to pat Emma's cheek approvingly before launching into a story that made Carlos laugh so hard he nearly spilled his wine.

When the food arrived—platters of grilled vegetables, calamari, glossy olives, and thick slices of bread—Miguel turned his attention to serving Rosie, watching her reactions with quiet pleasure.

"Is it what you hoped for?" he asked softly.

"Better," she said, and was startled by how much she meant it.

As the plates were cleared and fresh bottles of wine appeared, the mood grew even lighter. Maria caught herself laughing so freely she barely recognised the sound.

At one point, Emma leaned back in her chair, shading her eyes with her hand. "You know," she said, "I don't actually want to go home."

Rosie reached for her hand across the table. "Me neither."

Carlos smiled. "Then stay. At least a little longer."

Miguel tilted his head, his thumb brushing gently against Rosie's wrist. "We haven't even begun to show you the good places yet."

Maria felt her heart lift, weightless and a little reckless. She glanced at Emma, then at Rosie, and saw the same glimmer of possibility in their eyes.

"Well," Maria said, lifting her glass, "to adventures we didn't know we needed."

"To new stories," Miguel added.

They clinked glasses in a chorus of laughter and the quiet, unspoken understanding that life was too short to keep waiting for permission to be happy.

THE COUNTDOWN

The morning of the blue door visit dawned with a clarity that felt almost scripted. The sky was a flawless dome of blue, the air already warming with the promise of afternoon heat. Maria lay in bed for a while, staring at the ceiling, her heart beating in that uneven, fluttery rhythm she associated with exams and first dates.

At exactly seven o'clock, church bells began their measured chiming from the village square. She sat up, pressed her palms to her cheeks, and tried to steady herself. Today. After all the weeks of guessing and searching, *today* they would stand in front of the door in Lisa's photograph.

She could hear Rosie and Emma talking somewhere near the kitchen, their voices pitched higher than usual. When she appeared in the doorway, still in her nightdress, she found them sitting at the table with their phones, their coffee, and a handwritten schedule in Emma's neat print.

"Good, you're up," Rosie said, looking relieved. "We have a plan."

Maria raised an eyebrow. "A plan?"

"For the morning," Emma explained. "We can't just sit here staring at the clock until four. We'll go mad."

"So we're going to the Sóller market," Rosie continued, tapping the list. "Get a proper lunch, look at something colourful, pretend we're not obsessing."

Maria set her hands on the back of a chair and studied them. Both women looked slightly wild around the eyes, the way they did whenever they were determined to manage their nerves through activity.

"All right," she said after a beat. "But you both know we're going to check the time every five minutes."

Emma gave a rueful laugh. "Yes. But at least we'll be doing it somewhere picturesque."

They dressed quickly, moving through the villa in a kind of choreographed urgency. Maria chose a linen dress she hadn't yet worn—a soft cream that made her look improbably serene, even as her hands shook while she buttoned it.

As she came back through the sitting room, she caught her reflection in the tall mirror. For a second, she barely recognised herself: her posture straighter, her face a little pink with anticipation. She thought of what Carlos had said about living as if she deserved joy, and some tender, defiant part of her believed it might be true.

By nine o'clock, they were climbing into the little yellow Citroën, which Carlos had loaned them for the day. A note on the dashboard read, *Enjoy your adventure. Call me if you need anything.*

Rosie read it aloud, her voice softening. "He's a good man," she said, folding the note and tucking it into Maria's handbag.

Maria pretended not to notice the way Emma looked at her, eyebrows lifted, but she couldn't keep the smile off her lips.

It took longer than they'd planned to reach Sóller. Traffic was thick with delivery vans and holidaymakers, and every red light felt like a personal affront. Rosie kept glancing at the dashboard clock, tapping her foot on the floor.

"We have six hours," Maria reminded her as they finally pulled into a parking space. "Even if we get lost, we'll be back in plenty of time."

"That's what you say now," Rosie grumbled, hauling her bag over her shoulder. "Just wait until it's two o'clock and we're trapped in some café twenty miles away."

Emma rolled her eyes. "We're going to be fine."

But as they walked through the arched entrance to the market, Maria felt her own pulse quicken again. Each moment brought them closer to something she wasn't sure she was ready to see.

THE MARKET WAS a riot of colour and scent and human voices. Even in her nervous state, Maria couldn't help feeling captivated.

Tomatoes the size of grapefruits gleamed in pyramids beside braids of garlic and piles of glossy aubergines. Stalls overflowed with wildflowers, honey in glass jars, woven baskets, wheels of cheese, bundles of fresh herbs. The air smelled of ripe peaches and warm bread.

"This was a good idea," Emma said under her breath, sketchbook already out. "It feels...alive."

Rosie was less convinced. She was clutching her phone in one hand, checking the time between every stall.

"Still four hours to go," she announced at one point, voice strained.

Maria steered her toward a stand selling hand-painted tiles. "Then let's make them count," she said, surprising herself with the firmness in her tone.

They drifted among the vendors, stopping when Emma needed to draw or when Maria's curiosity won out over her impatience. Rosie gradually relaxed enough to admire a stack of linen tablecloths embroidered with pomegranates.

When a vendor offered them slices of melon so sweet it tasted like summer itself, Maria felt something in her ease, as though Lisa's spirit was somewhere among them, urging them to live instead of merely endure.

They bought olives, flatbreads, a wedge of manchego, and three paper cones filled with sugared almonds. Rosie checked the clock again.

"Eleven-forty," she reported. "We still have time. Barely."

Emma wiped her hands on her skirt and looked around with an artist's hunger. "Five more minutes," she pleaded. "I want to sketch that fishmonger."

"Five," Rosie agreed, holding up her hand like a referee. "No more."

Maria wandered a little apart, letting the crowd eddy around her. She didn't realise how long she'd stood staring at a display of antique postcards until a warm voice spoke at her shoulder.

"I thought I might find you here."

She turned, and there was Carlos, holding a small bundle wrapped in brown paper. He looked tired in the way of someone who had been working since dawn, but his smile was easy and sure.

"How did you know?" she asked.

"I didn't," he said. "But I hoped."

He handed her the bundle. Inside was a tiny blue tile painted with a white flower.

"For luck," he said.

She pressed it to her palm, feeling the smooth glaze, the weight of it. "Thank you," she whispered.

He stepped a little closer. "Are you all right?"

She nodded, though her throat felt too tight to answer properly.

"Do you want me to come with you this afternoon?"

She looked past him to where Rosie was waving urgently, clearly wanting her to come back before they lost track of time.

"I think…" Maria began, searching for her words. "I think we need to do it ourselves. But afterwards…"

"I'll be here," he said simply. "Whatever you need."

And he bent to kiss her cheek, so gently it made her eyes sting.

THEY LEFT the market just after noon. The car was hot as an oven when they climbed in. Rosie cranked down the window, fanning herself with the schedule.

"Three hours," she announced. "Three."

Emma tucked her sketchbook onto her lap. "How are we supposed to survive three more hours?"

Maria rested her head against the seat. "One minute at a time."

BACK AT THE VILLA, they spread their treasures on the kitchen table. The afternoon felt endless. They tried to distract themselves by making lunch, but every few minutes someone would check a phone or glance at the clock.

The gazpacho turned out watery. The tortilla collapsed in the middle. Rosie dropped an entire dish of olives on the floor and stood there laughing and crying in equal measure.

"We're hopeless," she said, wiping her eyes.

"No," Maria said, gathering the olives into a bowl. "We're just…somewhere else."

AT TWO O'CLOCK, the doorbell rang. Miguel stepped in carrying a paper bag from his restaurant.

"I thought you might need something edible," he said, holding it aloft like a peace offering.

Rosie let out a helpless laugh. "You're a saint."

He set the bag down, kissed her cheek, and looked around. "How are you all feeling?"

"Like we're about to be sick," Emma said honestly.

Miguel's gaze softened. "It's a good thing," he said gently. "To care enough that it makes you tremble."

They ate his food standing up, too restless to sit. Every bite felt unreal. At half past two, Maria slipped away to the terrace, needing air.

Carlos was there, leaning against the wall. He didn't say anything when she joined him. He just reached for her hand.

"I feel like I'm about to jump out of my skin," she confessed.

"I know," he murmured. "That means you're alive."

She turned her hand so their palms met fully. "Promise me you'll be here when we get back."

"I promise."

INSIDE, Rosie and Emma were gathering their bags with solemn ceremony. Rosie looked pale but determined.

Emma checked her phone. "Two fifty-five."

Maria took a breath that felt like the first one all day.

"All right," she said, her voice steadier than she felt. "Let's go find our blue door."

Miguel stepped forward, pressing a kiss to Rosie's temple. "We'll see you tonight," he said. "When it's done."

Carlos caught Maria's gaze, something bright and certain there. She didn't look away.

Then, without another word, the three women stepped into the afternoon heat, the little blue tile still warm in Maria's pocket, their hearts thundering with hope and fear and something that felt like love.

And together, they set out toward Valldemossa.

THE BLUE DOOR

*T*he drive to Valldemossa felt longer than any journey they'd taken since arriving in Spain. Maria couldn't remember a single word spoken after they turned off the coastal road. The three of them sat in the little Citroën with their hands tucked in their laps, eyes fixed on the landscape unspooling outside the windows—ochre stone terraces, dark cypresses, fat sheep grazing in patches of faded grass.

She kept her gaze on the mountains, trying to slow her breathing, but her heart insisted on hammering out a fast, relentless rhythm. She was conscious of everything: the warmth of the seat beneath her, the faint squeak of the suspension, the salt-laden breeze creeping in through the cracked window.

Rosie's phone buzzed in the cup holder, startling them all. She picked it up as though it might detonate. "A text," she whispered. "From Miguel. He says he's thinking of us."

Emma let out a sound that was half-laugh, half-sob. "Tell him thank you. Tell him we're about to pass out from nerves."

Maria's fingers tightened around her handbag. Inside was the photograph—creased now from too many hands, too many hopeful comparisons. She could picture Lisa in it without looking: standing straight and proud in front of the blue door, her chin lifted, her eyes fierce and amused. As though she'd been daring the camera—and maybe the world—to underestimate her.

At last, Carlos slowed the car. The tyres crunched over gravel, and then they were turning up a narrow lane lined with old stone walls. Wild rosemary spilled through the gaps, sending a bright, resinous scent into the warm afternoon air.

"This is it," Rosie murmured.

Maria didn't answer. She was too busy memorising every detail.

They rounded a bend, and the house came into view—a long, low building made of pale golden stone that glowed in the sunlight. A stand of olive trees cast flickering shadows over the roof tiles, their leaves whispering in the breeze. In front of the house, a small garden bloomed in a riot of colour: geraniums, bougainvillea, tall spires of lavender nodding in the heat.

And there, exactly where it had always been in the photograph, stood the door.

It was a shade of blue that defied easy description—something deeper than sky, lighter than navy, softened by time and weather into a colour that felt alive. The paint had cracked in places, revealing slivers of wood beneath, and a simple iron handle shone dully in the afternoon light.

No one spoke. Maria felt her chest contract, as though her heart had decided to fold itself into a tight, protective knot.

Carlos switched off the engine. For a moment, no one moved.

Rosie cleared her throat. "If I get out of this car, I might never get back in."

Emma reached over and covered her hand. "If you stay in the car, you'll never forgive yourself."

A puff of wind sent petals skittering across the gravel, and

Maria thought—absurdly, fiercely—that Lisa would have loved the drama of it.

"Come on," she said quietly. "We've come too far to stop now."

She was the first to open her door. Her legs wobbled as she climbed out, and she pressed her hand to the warm metal of the car to steady herself. The air smelled of rosemary and dust, and something sweeter she couldn't place.

The others followed, closing their doors with a series of soft, final clicks.

They stood together at the edge of the garden, staring at the house. Maria became aware that she was holding her breath. She let it out slowly, trying to remind herself she was still alive, still here, still herself.

Emma was blinking too fast, her sketchbook clutched tight to her chest. Rosie had gone pale, the freckles on her nose standing out like constellations.

Maria felt a wave of tenderness for them both—these women who had carried her through grief and confusion and now stood beside her at the end of the trail.

"Do you want a moment?" Carlos asked gently. He hadn't left the car yet. He sat with his arm draped over the wheel, his face patient, understanding.

Maria shook her head. "I don't think there's any preparing for this."

She took a step forward. The gravel shifted under her sandals. Another step.

At the edge of the path, she paused and turned back. "Come with me," she said to Rosie and Emma. "All of you."

Carlos got out then, crossing to stand just behind her. She didn't need to look to feel the steadiness of his presence.

Together, they walked up the path toward the blue door.

Maria let her fingertips brush the wood. It was warm from

the sun, and faintly rough under her skin. For one suspended moment, she forgot about everyone else and closed her eyes.

She could see Lisa as she'd been at twenty-five: brash, unstoppable, wearing a thrifted leather jacket and a grin that could dismantle your best defences in seconds. She could hear her voice—low, amused: *Honestly, Maria, you think too much. Just do the thing. Whatever it is, do it.*

Her throat closed around a sound she couldn't name.

When she opened her eyes, Rosie was beside her, pressing her palm to the door as if to test whether it was real. Emma stood a little apart, sketchbook clutched to her chest like a talisman.

"It's exactly the same," Rosie whispered. "Even the handle. Even the number."

Maria nodded. "It's like she just stepped inside for a minute."

They stood there in silence. The house seemed to be listening, patient and unhurried, as if it had been expecting them all along.

At last, Emma spoke. "What if we're wrong?" Her voice was small, fragile. "What if this isn't her place at all?"

Maria drew a shaky breath. "Then we thank the people here and keep looking. But I don't think we're wrong."

Rosie squared her shoulders. "No. Me neither."

The door opened before they could knock.

A woman stood there, framed in the shadowed doorway. She was perhaps in her fifties, with weathered skin, strong shoulders, and hair bound back in a simple knot. Her eyes, the same blue as the door behind her, moved from one of them to the next, as though cataloguing their expressions.

"Good afternoon," she said in accented English. "I am Marisol Mendoza. You called yesterday?"

Maria's voice deserted her.

Emma stepped in, her words too fast. "Yes—thank you— thank you for letting us come. We didn't know who else to ask."

Marisol studied them for a long, thoughtful moment. Then she stepped back, holding the door wide. "You'd better come in."

The cool air of the house washed over them as they crossed the threshold. Maria felt her knees almost give way with relief.

Inside, the front hall was simple and clean, with terracotta tiles and pale plaster walls. Sunlight pooled on the floor in a golden square. On a narrow table rested a chipped ceramic vase filled with wildflowers.

"You have come a long way," Marisol said quietly.

Maria found her voice at last. "Yes."

Marisol nodded. She gestured toward an archway that opened into what looked like a sitting room. "We can sit. You will tell me about your friend."

They followed her into a space that smelled of lavender and old wood. Through an open window, Maria glimpsed a court-yard shaded by fig trees. She sat on the edge of a sofa, feeling absurdly like a child waiting to be scolded.

Marisol settled into a chair opposite them, folding her hands. "Please," she said. "Tell me why you have come."

Rosie cleared her throat. "We're here because of a photo-graph. Because of a woman we loved. She was adopted from Mallorca in the late sixties. We think—" She stopped, swal-lowed. "We hope this was her home."

Marisol listened without interruption, her gaze steady.

Maria reached into her bag and drew out the photograph. She held it out with both hands.

Marisol took it delicately, as though it might shatter. She studied it in the hush that followed.

At last, she looked up. "I remember her," she said simply. "Her name was Elisa. She was here for three years."

Emma let out a tiny, broken sound and covered her mouth with her hand.

Rosie pressed her palms together in front of her lips, tears sliding freely down her cheeks.

Maria closed her eyes and let her head drop forward. Relief flooded her so completely it left her lightheaded.

"Thank you," she whispered. "Thank you for remembering."

Marisol set the photograph gently on the table. "You have come to bring her home," she said.

Maria looked up. "Yes."

Outside, the wind stirred the fig leaves, sending cool shadows rippling across the walls.

In that moment, Maria felt something in her uncoil—something that had been bound tight for too long. They had found the blue door. They had found the place where Lisa began.

And for the first time since she'd died, Maria felt sure that Lisa knew.

REFLECTIONS ON THE
BLUE DOOR

They left the house with the blue door in a hush so complete that it seemed almost sacrilegious to break it. The street lay before them in the mellow late afternoon light, stone facades glowing golden, the air thick with the smell of rosemary and woodsmoke.

None of them spoke as they walked. Maria kept her gaze fixed on the uneven cobbles, trying to hold together the fragile sense of reality. She could feel the others moving around her—Rosie shifting her tote bag higher on her shoulder, Emma fiddling with the little notebook she'd been clutching like a talisman all day—but it was as though they were all under glass, separate from the ordinary world.

They'd found it. After all the false starts and guesswork, all the dead ends and hopeful leads, they'd actually stood in front of the blue door from Lisa's photograph. It was real. It existed.

But as the knowledge settled into her bones, Maria discovered that certainty could be as destabilising as doubt.

She tried to catch Rosie's eye, to say something—anything—to puncture the charged quiet. But Rosie was staring straight ahead, her face unreadable. Beside her, Emma was blinking rapidly, as though she was determined not to let tears fall in public.

It was Emma who finally broke the silence.

"Did you ever think," she said hoarsely, "that finding it would make me feel worse?"

Maria stopped walking. The question hung between them like smoke.

Rosie turned, her brow furrowed. "Worse how?"

Emma pressed her palm to her forehead. "I don't know. Like…it proves she was real. And I still can't believe she's gone."

The ache in Maria's chest intensified. She reached out and took Emma's free hand. It was cold, trembling.

"I know," she said quietly. "I feel it too."

They stood there, three English women in the middle of a sunstruck Majorcan street, and let the moment be what it was— complicated, unpolished, utterly human.

THEY DIDN'T HAVE the energy to find a taxi or even to remember the name of the café Carlos had pointed out as having the best almond cake in the valley. So they walked, past shops with bright ceramic house numbers, past a florist arranging yellow lilies in a bucket, past a boy kicking a deflated football down an alley.

The ordinariness of it all made Maria's throat burn. Life continued whether you were ready or not.

She realised she was clutching Lisa's photo so tightly that her hand ached. She forced herself to loosen her grip, smoothing the edge where it had begun to fray.

"Do you remember," she said, her voice scratchy, "when she told us she'd always wanted to live somewhere warm?"

Rosie blinked. "Yes. She said she was going to buy a white-washed house on a hill and fill it with stray cats."

"She said she'd never wear shoes again," Emma added, a small, bewildered smile pulling at her mouth.

Maria looked up at the sky, fighting tears. "She said she wanted to learn Spanish so she could flirt properly."

They all laughed then—thin, uneven laughter, but real.

BY THE TIME they reached the little square where Carlos had parked, the shadows had stretched long across the paving stones. The light was turning the colour of apricots.

Carlos was leaning against the Citroën, arms folded, watching them approach with that quiet attentiveness Maria was beginning to recognise as his particular form of gentleness.

He didn't ask how it had gone. He simply opened the passenger door, helped them inside one by one, and drove without comment.

No one spoke on the journey back.

THE VILLA WAS HUSHED when they returned, as though the walls themselves understood something momentous had happened. Maria kicked off her sandals and padded into the kitchen. The air smelled of lemons and cool tile.

"I'm going to open the wine," she called over her shoulder. "I don't care that it's only six o'clock."

"Make it two bottles," Rosie said, appearing in the doorway. She dropped her bag onto a chair. "I can't feel my legs."

"I'm having gin," Emma announced. "And if you judge me, I'll throw you in the pool."

THEY GATHERED AROUND THE TABLE, glasses in hand.

For a few minutes, no one tried to fill the space. The silence felt necessary, like the pause after a funeral service before everyone remembered how to breathe again.

Maria reached out and touched the folded photograph at the centre of the table.

"She was really here," she said softly. "She was a little girl, standing on those tiles."

Rosie let out a shaky exhale. "I keep thinking about her running down that corridor. The woman said she always ran everywhere. That she was never still."

Emma rubbed her eyes. "She must have been scared, sometimes. But she was always so…alive."

The memory came to Maria unbidden: Lisa, twenty-five, luminous in a yellow sundress, sitting cross-legged on the floor of Maria's kitchen with a bottle of cheap prosecco and a stack of wedding invitations.

"You don't have to marry Richard, you know," she'd said, her eyes bright with mischief and concern. "You could run away with me. I have a little red suitcase and absolutely no sense of direction."

Maria had laughed and said, "What would we do?"

"Whatever we like," Lisa had replied. "Isn't that the point?"

She pressed her knuckles to her mouth, blinking hard.

"I think she'd be glad we found it," she said when she could trust her voice again.

Rosie nodded. "And annoyed that she couldn't be here to see us make fools of ourselves in the process."

"She'd be smug," Emma agreed. "She'd say she knew we'd do it all along."

THEY POURED MORE WINE. At some point, Emma disappeared and came back with her sketchbook. She flipped it open to a fresh page and began drawing the doorway they'd stood in front of that afternoon.

"Are you sure you want to do that now?" Rosie asked gently.

Emma didn't look up. "If I don't, I'll forget the way the light fell on the threshold. The way it looked like...like an invitation."

Maria swallowed. "An invitation to what?"

"To find out who she was," Emma murmured. "And who we are without her."

THE HOURS SLID BY, measured in glasses of wine and the soft scratch of Emma's pencil.

At some point, Maria rose and fetched her journal from her bedroom. She hadn't opened it in days, afraid that putting words to paper would make everything too real. But now, the need to write was stronger than her fear.

She sat on the terrace under the string of fairy lights and let her pen move:

Tonight I feel closer to Lisa than I have in years. Closer and further away. It's as if finding the door gave her back to us and took her away again in the same breath. I don't know what to do with that.

Inside, she could hear Rosie's voice drifting through the open window.

"Remember when she got caught in that affair with the MP?" Rosie was saying. "God, she thought she was so discreet. Until the tabloids found out."

Emma giggled. "She hid in the toilets for three hours. Climbed out the window."

Maria smiled, tears blurring her writing.

She was so alive. So unapologetic. Maybe that's why losing her feels like losing some part of myself I hadn't realised was still capable of courage.

AFTER A WHILE, Carlos came back. He brought fresh bread and cheese and the calm presence that Maria was coming to rely on.

He didn't ask what they were talking about. He simply poured a glass of water for each of them and set it down without comment.

"Will you stay?" Maria asked him quietly as he turned to go.

He looked at her, searching her face for a moment. Then he pulled out a chair and sat down beside her.

"If you want me to," he said simply.

She didn't know how to say what she felt. That she was afraid, and grateful, and too raw to pretend any of it was simple.

Instead, she put her hand over his on the table. He turned it palm up and threaded his fingers through hers.

For a long time, they didn't speak.

LATER, after Emma had gone to bed and Rosie was asleep in the chair by the fire, Maria stayed up. She thought about the little girl Lisa had been. The teenager who'd convinced them all to skip lectures and go to Rome on a whim. The woman who'd known she was dying but insisted on living anyway.

I'm not ready to let you go, she thought.

She imagined Lisa laughing, rolling her eyes.

You don't have to let me go, her voice seemed to say. *Just don't stop moving forward.*

WHEN THE MOON was high over the hills and the villa had gone still, Maria closed her journal and whispered into the quiet:

"Thank you. For the adventure. For the reminder that life doesn't end just because someone you love isn't here to see it."

She felt something loosen inside her chest, like a knot coming undone.

Tomorrow, there would be more questions. More decisions.

But tonight, there was this:

The certainty that love had been here. That it had mattered.

And that was enough.

LATER THAT NIGHT, when the others had finally drifted off to bed, Rosie sat alone in the kitchen, her phone clutched in her hand like a lifeline she didn't know whether to grab or toss away.

Her thumb hovered over her daughter's number. She knew if she called now—if she said, *"Darling, there's someone I want you to meet,"*—it would all become real.

Real in a way that suddenly felt frightening.

Miguel was…God, he was wonderful. The kind of man she'd stopped believing in. Kind, attentive, self-deprecating in that quiet, Spanish way that made her feel seen without feeling inspected.

But what would Daisy say? Or George, who'd always looked at her with that slightly pitying affection, as though she were a harmless eccentric destined to remain alone?

What would they think when she told them she'd met a man who owned a restaurant and kissed her in broad daylight, who called her *preciosa* like it was the most obvious word in the world?

What if they thought she'd lost her mind?

She set the phone down and pressed her palms to her eyes.

It's my life, she thought fiercely. *They don't get to vote.*

But the conviction felt flimsy, like a paper lantern in a windstorm.

EMMA'S DOUBTS

*E*mma couldn't sleep.

She slipped from her room and out to the terrace, carrying her sketchbook. The night was velvet-soft, threaded with jasmine and the hush of distant waves.

She settled into the wicker chair, drawing her knees up to her chest. The paper felt cool against her fingertips.

She tried to sketch the view—rooftops silvered in moonlight, the dark mass of the mountains beyond—but her pencil faltered.

Her thoughts kept circling back to England.

To the narrow terraced house with its damp hallway and the kitchen clock that ticked away her evenings. To her daughter, who called twice a week to check she was eating properly. To the life she'd left behind so easily it almost frightened her.

What if this is just running away?

She pressed her thumb to the page, smudging the graphite.

Behind her, the door creaked open. Maria stepped out, wrapped in a shawl.

"You couldn't sleep either?"

Emma shook her head. "I'm all right. Go back in."

But Maria came and sat beside her, hands folded in her lap.

For a long time, neither of them spoke.

Finally, Emma set down her pencil. "Do you ever think… we're being selfish?"

Maria tilted her head. "Selfish?"

"Running off to Spain. Leaving everything behind. Everyone."

Maria considered this. "Sometimes," she admitted. "But then I remember how many years I spent doing what everyone else thought was best."

Emma looked away. "My daughter said I deserve this. But I keep wondering—what if I'm needed and I'm not there?"

Maria reached over and covered Emma's hand with her own. "Then they will learn how strong they are without you."

Tears burned behind Emma's eyes.

"It doesn't feel brave," she whispered. "It feels…self-indulgent."

"It's both," Maria said gently. "Sometimes, the bravest thing is to choose yourself."

THEY SAT in silence as the sky began to pale at the edges.

When Emma finally spoke, her voice was steadier.

"Tomorrow, we go to the blue door."

Maria nodded. "And after that?"

"I don't know," Emma admitted. "But maybe that's all right."

THE FIRST BIRDS began to sing. Emma closed her sketchbook and let herself believe that uncertainty might be its own kind of freedom.

THE LETTER

*M*aria was in the garden early, before the sun had lifted fully above the tiled rooftops. The villa was still and cool, the only sound the sleepy cooing of doves perched in the fig tree. She clipped back a stubborn tangle of bougainvillea, feeling the quiet in her chest like an ache.

Yesterday had left her drained in a way she hadn't expected. Standing in that small bedroom with the blue shutters thrown wide, she'd felt both closer to Lisa and further away than ever before. She could still see the child's dress in the wardrobe, the blue gingham soft with age. Could still feel the hush that had gathered around them as they read the old ledger with Lisa's name in small, neat letters.

Not afraid.

Maria pressed her lips together. If she closed her eyes, she could almost hear Lisa's voice in the courtyard behind her— laughing, teasing, dismissing sentiment with a flick of her hand. You're being maudlin, Maria. Life's for living.

The trouble was, Maria wasn't sure she knew how to start again.

A floorboard creaked behind her, and she turned to see

Emma standing barefoot in the kitchen doorway. Her hair was a dishevelled halo, her expression soft with sleep.

"I thought you'd be out here," Emma said, rubbing her arms against the morning chill. "Couldn't sleep?"

Maria shook her head. "I kept seeing that little room. The way the light fell across the floorboards. As if she'd just stepped out and might walk back in at any moment."

Emma came to stand beside her, looking out across the low stone wall to the olive grove. The trees shimmered silver in the dawn, ancient and indifferent. "I know. I kept thinking about her first night there. What she must have felt."

"Lonely," Maria murmured. "So small, and already so determined to be brave."

They stood in silence, letting the new day wrap itself around them. Emma slipped her hand through Maria's and squeezed.

"You know," Emma said after a while, "we came here to give her a resting place. But sometimes it feels like she's the one giving us something."

Maria swallowed the sudden thickness in her throat. "What do you mean?"

Emma tilted her head, considering. "Permission. To want more than we allowed ourselves. To be...unsettled. Curious. Alive."

Maria let out a breath that felt suspiciously close to a sob. "She always was the brave one."

Inside the kitchen, they found Rosie already dressed, her hair pulled up in a loose knot, flipping through her notebook. She looked up and smiled. "I was about to make coffee. You both look like you need it."

They settled around the table while Rosie filled the moka pot, the comforting hiss of the burner filling the room. Maria watched the ritual—grind the beans, measure the water, set it all carefully in place—and felt something loosen inside her. Even in uncertainty, there were small, sustaining routines.

"Any news from your lot?" Emma asked, nodding at the phone beside Rosie's notebook.

Rosie snorted. "Three missed calls from my sister, one text from my nephew saying Mum, when are you coming home, and a voicemail from my ex-husband that I haven't listened to yet. So, the usual."

Maria raised her eyebrows. "You're not tempted to call back?"

"God, no." Rosie slid the phone further away. "I've decided the world can wait. At least until I've had coffee."

They were halfway through their second cups when the low rumble of an engine drifted through the open window. Maria glanced up sharply. She knew that sound by now—the hopeful rattle of Carlos's old Citroën as it made the climb up to the villa.

She felt something flutter in her chest that she did her best to ignore.

A moment later, the front door swung open, and Carlos stepped into the kitchen, hat in hand. His face was serious, but his eyes warmed when they met hers.

"Forgive the intrusion," he said, his voice low. "I wouldn't come so early, but—well. I thought you'd want this as soon as possible."

Maria pushed back her chair, her heart giving an unhelpful thump. "What is it?"

Carlos hesitated, then stepped forward and set a small envelope on the table. It was yellowed, the flap sealed with an old-fashioned blob of blue wax.

"I went back to see Marisol first thing," he explained. "She found this in a drawer last night, after you'd gone. She asked me to bring it to you."

Maria stared at the envelope. It looked so ordinary, so unassuming. But her hands were already trembling.

Emma leaned forward, her eyes wide. "What is it?"

"A letter," Carlos said quietly. "From the doctor who cared

for Lisa. He left it with the family in case…in case someone ever came looking."

No one moved. The cicadas had started up in the garden, their chorus rising and falling in the hush that fell around the table.

Rosie let out a slow breath. "Well," she said. "That feels like something we should read."

Maria reached for the envelope but stopped, her fingertips hovering above it. "I don't know if I can."

Carlos laid a gentle hand on her shoulder. "Then let one of us."

Emma slid the envelope closer. She examined the seal as if it might disintegrate under her touch, then looked up. "If no one objects…I'll read it aloud."

Maria nodded, unable to speak.

Emma slipped a thumbnail under the wax and lifted the flap. Inside was a single sheet of thick cream paper, folded in thirds. She drew it out and unfolded it with slow care.

Her voice was steady as she began.

To Whomever Comes,

If you hold this letter, it means you are searching for Elisa.

I cannot tell you where she went after she left this house. But I can tell you who she was when she was here.

Elisa arrived in the winter of 1967, small and watchful. She did not cry, though many children did. Instead, she looked at me as if to measure my worth.

She had suffered much in her short life. But she did not wear her sorrow like a wound. Rather, it lay coiled inside her—a tension in the way she held herself, a wariness that only softened with time.

I came every fortnight to check the children's health. Most appointments were routine—measuring growth, treating coughs, recording weight. But with Elisa, there was always more to observe.

She learned quickly. She understood more than she said. And when she did speak, her words were precise and startling.

My wife sometimes accompanied me. She brought biscuits for the children and read them stories while I worked. She told me that Elisa was the most beautiful child she had ever seen. Not for her face, though she was lovely, but for her gravity.

"She looks as if she has already survived something," my wife said once. "And perhaps she has."

In time, Elisa began to trust. I remember the first time she reached for my hand of her own accord. It was Christmas, and I had brought small gifts—a carved wooden donkey for each child. She took hers and looked up at me with an expression I have never forgotten. As if, just for a moment, she believed she might be safe.

If you are the ones who loved her later, I hope this comforts you. She was not alone here. She was cared for.

And she was unforgettable.

In respect and remembrance,

Dr. Sebastià Alemany

When Emma's voice broke, she pressed her knuckles to her mouth, her shoulders shaking.

Rosie reached across the table, closing her hand over Emma's.

Maria sat back, her vision swimming. She lifted her own hand to her cheek and was startled to find it wet.

"She was cared for," she whispered. "That's all I ever wanted to know."

Carlos was very still beside her. When she turned her face toward him, she saw his own eyes were damp.

"She was never lost," he said softly. "Only moving forward."

The kitchen felt full—of old grief and new understanding, of relief and sorrow so intertwined they couldn't be separated.

Maria drew in a breath and let it out in a long, uneven sigh. "Thank you," she said, her voice husky. "For bringing it."

Carlos inclined his head. "It was an honour."

Emma folded the letter carefully along its creases, then slipped it back into the envelope. She tied the blue ribbon around it again with fingers that were steadier than Maria expected.

Rosie blew out a slow breath. "I feel...lighter. Is that strange?"

"No," Maria said, surprising herself with how sure she felt. "I feel it too."

They sat in silence, the letter resting between them like a benediction.

After a while, Carlos shifted. "I'll go," he said, though he didn't stand. "Unless you'd rather I stay."

Maria looked at him, feeling her heart lift and ache all at once. "Stay," she said softly. "Please."

He nodded, reaching across to take her hand in his.

THE DAY UNFOLDED GENTLY after that.

They carried the letter into the sitting room and set it on the low table beside the urn that held Lisa's ashes. Rosie brewed more coffee. Emma opened all the windows so the breeze could wander in and stir the curtains.

For a time, no one needed to talk. Maria sat with her feet tucked beneath her, watching the pale linen ripple, and let herself simply be. No past to regret. No future to fear. Only this moment, strange and luminous and real.

In the early afternoon, they shared a simple lunch—bread and olives, a wedge of Manchego, peaches so ripe their juices ran down their wrists. The conversation drifted from memory to speculation, from quiet laughter to thoughtful silence.

Emma spoke of her art classes at the community centre, of how the children's paintings had more courage in them than anything she'd created in years.

Rosie described the way Miguel had kissed her under the orange trees, and how she hadn't felt embarrassed to be seen wanting something.

Maria listened, her heart full and tender, and wondered if Lisa was somewhere watching them. Approving. Maybe a little smug.

LATE IN THE AFTERNOON, when the sun was a soft gold over the hills, Maria fetched her journal and sat under the fig tree.

She turned to a fresh page and set her pen to it.

I thought this would feel like an ending.

But it doesn't.

It feels like the place a story takes a breath before the next chapter.

She paused, lifting her eyes to the sky, where swallows dipped and wheeled.

Maybe that's what she wanted for us. Not closure. But courage.

The words felt right. When she looked up, she found Emma watching her from the kitchen doorway, her face solemn and bright all at once.

"Tomorrow?" Emma asked.

Maria nodded. "Tomorrow."

Tomorrow, they would walk to the grove.

Tomorrow, they would say the last of the words that needed saying.

And after that, there would be time to find out who they were becoming.

THE FESTIVAL

he next morning dawned low and grey, the sky streaked with pale cloud that looked as if it had been combed into place. Maria had slept badly. She had woken again and again to the memory of Carlos's voice, gentle and pained: *I just want you to believe this could be real.*

When she finally gave up on sleep, she dressed quietly and carried her sandals to the kitchen. She paused on the threshold, steeling herself for whatever expression might be waiting on Rosie's face. Concern. Sympathy. Worse—pity.

But when she stepped inside, she found Rosie standing at the counter, frowning over a small battered saucepan. She looked up and said, quite calmly, "I'm trying to make hot chocolate."

Maria blinked. "At six in the morning?"

"I couldn't sleep," Rosie said. She stirred the pot briskly, her hair escaping its clip in wild curls. "I thought, What would make me feel better? And the answer was sugar."

Emma appeared behind her, her robe belted tight and her face wan with exhaustion. "I second the sugar plan," she muttered, sinking into a chair. "I feel like I've been scrubbed raw."

Maria crossed to the table and sat heavily. "Me too."

For a while, no one spoke. The only sound was the rhythmic scrape of Rosie's spoon and the slow, steady drip of the tap that no one had ever quite fixed.

At last, Rosie set the saucepan down and looked at them both. "I don't know about you," she said, her voice surprisingly clear, "but I don't want to spend another day crying."

Emma lifted her chin. "Agreed."

Maria felt something flicker in her chest—a tiny, fragile spark of relief. "So what do we do instead?"

Rosie squared her shoulders. "We do something ordinary. Or something outrageous. Or something so beautiful it feels like the opposite of grief."

Emma reached for her hand. "Like what?"

But before Rosie could answer, a knock sounded at the door.

Maria's heart stuttered. For one impossible moment, she thought it might be Lisa herself—some last impossible twist in a story already full of them.

But when she opened the door, it was Carlos.

He looked tired. His hair was mussed, as if he had run a hand through it too many times. But he smiled—a tentative, hopeful curve of his mouth—and lifted a hand in greeting.

"I'm sorry," he said softly. "I know I'm early."

Maria swallowed, her fingers tightening on the edge of the door. "It's all right."

For a moment, neither of them moved. Then Rosie's voice called from the kitchen, brisk and bright. "You might as well come in. We're making hot chocolate and feeling sorry for ourselves."

Carlos hesitated, then stepped inside. He looked at Maria, and something passed between them—an understanding that they were still in the middle of it. Still finding their way.

He glanced around the kitchen, taking in the sight of the

three women in their rumpled clothes, their tired faces, the saucepan of chocolate steaming gently on the counter.

"You look…" He trailed off, searching for the right word.

"Like hell," Emma supplied dryly.

His mouth quirked. "I was going to say determined."

Rosie straightened, her jaw set. "We are."

He nodded once. "Good."

They settled around the table with mugs of rich, bittersweet chocolate. Maria felt the warmth seep into her hands, her chest loosening by increments.

At last, Carlos cleared his throat. "There's something I came to say," he began carefully. "And something I came to ask."

Maria braced herself.

"I meant what I said last night," he told her, his gaze steady. "I don't expect an answer. Not yet. Not about anything." He paused. "But I do want you to know that however long it takes —however long you need—I'll wait."

Something in her chest cracked, delicate as spun sugar. She set her mug down before she spilled it.

"Thank you," she whispered.

He nodded, once, as though they'd agreed on something weighty and necessary.

Then he looked around the table. "And the question I came to ask is this: Would you like to come to the festival in Sóller tonight?"

Emma frowned. "A festival?"

He smiled faintly. "The Feast of Sant Bartomeu. Lanterns, music, fireworks. I thought—it might be good to…celebrate."

Rosie looked up sharply. "Celebrate? After everything?"

Carlos met her gaze without flinching. "Sometimes celebration is the best way to honour someone."

No one spoke for a long moment.

Then Emma drew in a shaky breath. "I think she'd have liked that."

Maria looked at her friend, surprised.

Emma shrugged, her eyes bright. "Lisa never believed in wallowing."

Rosie pressed a hand to her mouth. A laugh escaped—a small, incredulous sound. "No," she said thickly. "She didn't."

Maria thought of Lisa's voice again, teasing and unafraid. *Life's for living, you idiot. Don't waste it on regrets.*

She closed her eyes. When she opened them, she nodded. "All right."

THEY SPENT the rest of the day in a strange, floating calm.

Rosie packed a small bag with spare scarves and a bright shawl she'd bought from a market stall. Emma tidied the kitchen with the restless energy of someone who couldn't bear to be still.

Maria retreated to her room. She sat on the edge of the bed for a long time, her hands resting on her knees.

At last, she opened the top drawer of her dresser. Nestled inside was the necklace she had brought from England—a simple silver chain with a locket she had never dared to open.

She lifted it out and pressed the cool metal to her lips. Then she fastened it around her neck.

If I'm going to say goodbye, she thought, *let me at least be brave about it.*

THE DRIVE into Sóller was quiet. The roads were narrow and winding, the stone houses turning pink in the sunset. In the back seat, Emma watched the hills flick past, her sketchbook balanced on her knees.

When they arrived, the town was already alive. Lanterns bobbed on long strings between the rooftops, each one painted with bright shapes—fish, flowers, birds. A band played in the square, the music fast and lilting.

Rosie drew in a long, unsteady breath. "It smells like every holiday I've ever wanted," she said, her voice unsteady.

Maria looked around. Children ran laughing through the crowd. Couples strolled arm in arm. Vendors called out their wares —grilled sardines, fresh churros, paper cones of sugared almonds.

For the first time in days, she felt her heart lift.

They made their way into the square. Emma peeled off to sketch the dancers, her face alight with concentration.

Maria and Rosie stood side by side, watching the swirl of colour and sound.

"I feel like we're intruding," Rosie murmured. "Like we're too sad to be here."

Maria shook her head. "I think…maybe this is the point. To remember that life goes on."

Rosie glanced at her, then looked away quickly. "God, Maria," she whispered. "I'm so tired of grieving."

Maria reached for her hand. "Me too."

SOMEWHERE BEHIND THEM, a voice called Rosie's name.

She turned. Miguel was threading his way through the crowd, his smile bright as the lanterns overhead.

"Dance with me," he said, his voice low and warm.

"I don't know the steps," she protested, even as her fingers found his.

"Then we'll invent them."

He led her into the throng, and she went—laughing, for the first time in days.

Maria watched them, her heart aching and tender all at once.

She felt a presence at her side and turned to find Carlos offering her a glass of sangria.

"They look happy," he said.

"They are," she said softly. "And they deserve it."

He studied her, his gaze steady. "So do you."

She hesitated. "I'm not sure I remember how."

He smiled, lifting her hand to his lips. "Then let me remind you."

THEY DANCED.

Maria didn't think she'd ever danced in a public square before. Certainly not in a foreign country, under a canopy of painted lanterns, with a man who looked at her as though she was a miracle.

At first, she was stiff. Afraid she'd trip over her own feet. But Carlos held her firmly, guiding her through the steps.

And then, slowly, something shifted.

She began to move with him, not thinking. Just feeling. The music thrummed through her bones, bright and insistent.

When the song ended, she was breathless, laughing. Carlos bent his head to kiss her cheek.

"You are braver than you know," he whispered.

Her throat closed. She turned away so he wouldn't see the tears in her eyes.

LATER, they sat on the low wall at the edge of the square. Rosie and Miguel were nearby, sharing roasted chestnuts. Emma returned with her sketchbook, her cheeks pink from excitement.

"Look," she said breathlessly.

She showed them the drawing—a portrait of the three of them standing in front of the blue door. A moment caught forever in graphite.

Maria felt something expand in her chest. A quiet, astonished happiness.

"It's beautiful," she whispered.

"It's us," Emma said simply.

THE FIREWORKS BEGAN JUST after ten. Bright blossoms of colour against the night sky.

Maria leaned her head on Carlos's shoulder. Rosie and Miguel stood close, their arms around each other.

And for the first time, Maria felt that she could breathe again.

THEY LEFT THE SQUARE SLOWLY, hands linked. The night was warm around them, scented with woodsmoke and spilled wine.

Halfway to the car, Carlos paused. He turned to face her.

"I know you're afraid," he said gently. "I am too."

Maria swallowed. "I know."

His thumb traced her cheekbone. "But I'd rather be afraid with you than safe without you."

She didn't answer. She only lifted her hand to his heart, feeling it beat under her palm.

For once, she didn't think about tomorrow. About what she owed her children. About how sensible women behaved.

She only thought: *I am alive.*

THE DOCTOR'S LETTER

$\mathcal{M}$aria was in the garden, pruning the lavender back to stubs, when she heard Rosie call from the terrace.

"Maria? You'd better come in—Carlos is here."

Her hands stilled on the secateurs. Something in Rosie's voice—an undertone of wonder, or maybe dread—made her stomach tighten. She pressed her palm flat over her heart, as if to keep it from leaping ahead of her thoughts.

Inside, Emma and Rosie were already standing by the kitchen table. Carlos hovered near the door, hat in hand, as though he hadn't quite decided whether he was staying.

"Is everything all right?" Maria asked, stepping over the threshold.

Carlos looked up. His eyes were bright, almost fevered. "I think so," he said. "Or—yes. I believe it is. I've just come from Valldemossa."

Maria felt her breath catch. "The house?"

"Yes." He lifted a small parcel wrapped in waxed paper. "Marisol was sorting through the last of her father's boxes and found this. She called me. She thought you would want it."

He set the bundle gently on the table. The paper was brittle with age, the edges folded back on themselves as though handled many times. A ribbon—pale blue, almost grey now—was tied around it in a careful bow.

Maria reached for the back of a chair to steady herself. "More records?"

Carlos hesitated. "Not records," he said softly. "Letters."

"Letters?" Emma echoed.

Carlos nodded. "From Lisa's old doctor. He used to visit the house regularly to check on the children. Apparently, before he retired, he wrote down everything he could remember about the ones who mattered most to him. He left them with Marisol's parents, just in case."

Emma let out a ragged breath. "Just in case someone came looking."

Maria pressed her hand over her mouth. In that moment, she felt the ground under her feet tilt. It was too much—too much loss, too much hope, too much of Lisa arriving again and again when she thought she'd said her last goodbye.

Rosie touched her elbow. "Do you want to sit?"

Maria nodded, and they eased her into a chair. She let her fingers rest against the cool wood of the table, needing something solid.

When she could trust her voice, she looked up at Carlos. "Thank you," she whispered.

His eyes softened. "It was never just a search," he said. "It was a homecoming."

Gently, he placed the letters in front of her. Then he stepped back, giving them space.

No one reached for the ribbon straight away. It felt almost indecent, this intimacy from a stranger long gone. Maria thought of all the years Lisa must have believed her beginnings were lost forever—and how a man she'd known only as a child had loved her enough to preserve them.

At last, Emma swallowed. "Should we read them?"

Rosie nodded, though her eyes glistened. "Yes. If you're ready."

Maria looked down at the blue ribbon. "I think," she said slowly, "I've been ready for a long time."

With trembling fingers, she untied the bow. The paper fell open in slow, delicate folds, revealing three letters stacked one atop the other. Their creases were deep, the ink faded but legible.

She picked up the first letter. In the upper corner, a neat hand had written a date: December 1964.

Maria met Emma's gaze. "Would you read it aloud?"

Emma drew in a slow breath. "Of course."

She took the letter with a care that made Maria's throat ache. Then she began to read.

To Whom It May Concern,

If you are reading this, it means that Lisa has left this place, as all children must. It is my hope that she left knowing she was cherished.

I first met her in December of 1967. She was so small she barely reached my knee, and she carried herself with a watchfulness that struck me immediately. I remember thinking she looked like a child who had already learned that the world did not owe her kindness.

But Lisa was more than her sadness. She was a determined little thing—curious, bright, stubborn. She had a way of sitting very still when you spoke to her, as if she were collecting every word to keep for later.

She loved music. If there was singing in the kitchen, she would drift closer, pretending not to listen. But her feet would tap. And when she thought no one was watching, she would hum along.

She loved to climb. I remember finding her on top of the henhouse once, waving as though it were the most natural place in the world.

And she loved stories. She never tired of hearing them—about the saints, about the villages, about the faraway cities she was certain she'd visit someday.

She was—she is—a child I have never forgotten.

If you loved her later in life, as I have no doubt you did, know this: she was loved first. By the people who held her when she was small. By the women who taught her to tie her shoes. By the old doctor who carried her on his shoulders the first time she saw snow.

May you find comfort in knowing she began her life surrounded by warmth.

With respect,

Dr. Sebastià Alemany

BY THE TIME Emma's voice fell quiet, no one was pretending they weren't crying. Maria pressed the back of her wrist to her mouth. Rosie's shoulders shook silently. Emma set the letter down and covered her face with her hands.

It was Maria who spoke first, her voice unsteady. "I don't know why it matters so much," she whispered, "but it does."

Rosie reached across the table and laid her palm over Maria's. "Because now we know she was never alone."

Maria nodded. She felt something loosen in her chest—a knot she hadn't even realised she'd been carrying.

Carlos cleared his throat gently. "There are two more."

Maria looked up. "Stay," she said, surprising herself. "Please."

He inclined his head. "Of course."

Emma picked up the second letter. "Do you want me to…?"

"Yes," Maria said.

Emma unfolded the paper. Her hands were steadier now.

MARCH 1967

121

Today Lisa asked me what the word "belonging" meant. She was six, and her Spanish had grown fluent enough to ask such questions.

I told her it meant to be part of something bigger than yourself. To have a place that was yours, and people who claimed you as theirs.

She frowned in that serious way she had, then said, "I don't think I belong anywhere."

I tried to explain that she belonged here, with us. That even if her life took her far away, this place would always be part of her story.

She seemed unconvinced. But later, I found her in the garden, her small hands pressed to the earth as though she were willing it to remember her.

If you are reading this, I hope she found the belonging she craved. I hope she learned that love makes its own roots.

Dr. Sebastià Alemany

MARIA FELT her tears spill over again. She covered her mouth with her hand and let the ache crest.

"She did," she whispered when she could speak. "She found it with us."

Rosie reached for her hand again, and Emma laid her palm on top. The three of them sat joined, their grief and their love intertwined.

After a long moment, Emma picked up the final letter. "Ready?"

Maria nodded. "Go on."

JULY 1969

Lisa left for England today.

She climbed into the car with her new family, wearing a blue dress my wife had made for her. She held her chin high, but her eyes were wide.

I stood by the gate and watched until the car disappeared around the bend. Then I went inside and sat at the kitchen table, unable to move.

My wife said she would be fine—that she was brave, that she was loved. And I knew she was right. But my heart ached in a way I could not explain.

There are some children you never forget.

If you are reading this, know that she took a piece of my heart with her.

Dr. Sebastià Alemany

WHEN EMMA'S voice trailed away, the kitchen fell into a silence as deep as any Maria had ever known. Even the cicadas outside seemed to have paused.

At last, Rosie exhaled. "She was loved," she said softly. "Everywhere she went."

Maria pressed her palm to the envelope that had held the letters. It felt warm from their hands. "I don't know why I ever doubted it."

Carlos shifted closer, just enough that their shoulders brushed. "Because you needed to see it written down."

Maria turned to him. "Thank you," she whispered.

He shook his head. "You found her story. I only helped carry it."

THEY SAT THERE until the light began to fade, talking in low voices about the girl Lisa had been and the woman she became. Maria found herself telling stories she hadn't thought of in years—the time Lisa insisted on camping in the garden in the middle of October, the night she danced alone under a summer storm.

By the time they stood to leave the table, the air had shifted. The grief was still there, but it had softened, threaded through with gratitude.

As the afternoon shadows lengthened, Emma excused herself. 'I need to prepare for tomorrow's class,' she said, but Maria saw something urgent in her eyes, a need to capture what she was feeling before it escaped.

At the community centre, Emma stood before her easel in the late afternoon light, surrounded by the cheerful chaos of children's art class.

She was demonstrating proper brush technique when little Ana, age seven, knocked over her water jar.

"Oh!" Ana cried, watching in horror as the murky water spread across her painting – a carefully drawn house with a garden.

"It's ruined!" She began to cry.

Emma reached for paper towels, but then stopped. The water had transformed Ana's precise little painting into something else entirely. The colors bled and merged, creating unexpected shadows, turning the rigid house into something that seemed to breathe.

"Wait," Emma said. "Look what you've made."

Ana sniffled. "It's all wrong now."

"Is it?" Emma knelt beside her. "Or is it just different than you planned?"

She watched Ana consider the painting with new eyes. Where before there had been careful lines, now there were suggestions of movement, of life beyond control.

"It looks like... like the house is dreaming," Ana said wonderingly.

That night, Emma stayed late in the studio. She set up a fresh canvas and, for the first time in decades, didn't sketch anything first. She just loaded her brush with paint and began.

She painted the feeling of standing before the blue door. Not the door itself, but the sensation – the tightness in her chest, the hope and fear tangled together, the weight of love for a friend who would never see what they'd found. She painted in blues that weren't sky or sea but the color of held breath, in whites that were the shade of unspoken words.

When she finally stepped back, her hands were shaking. The painting looked nothing like her usual careful landscapes. It was raw, emotional, technically imperfect. It was also the truest thing she'd ever created.

"Dios mío," Carmen said from the doorway. Emma hadn't heard her come in. "Emma, this is... this is extraordinary."

"It's a mess," Emma said, but she was smiling through her tears.

"It's honest," Carmen corrected. "This is what I've been waiting to see from you. This is art that matters."

BACK AT THE VILLA, Carlos rose to go, and Maria walked him to the door. He paused, studying her face in the last of the evening light.

"Are you all right?" he asked.

She surprised herself by smiling. "I think I'm better than I've been in a long time."

He bent to kiss her cheek, lingering just a moment. "Then I'm glad."

LATER, as she folded the letters back into their envelope, Maria realised something she hadn't understood before: She would always grieve Lisa. But grief, she saw now, was just another form of love. And love—true love—never ended.

It simply changed shape.

And in that knowledge, she felt—for the first time since the journey began—ready for whatever came next.

She looked up to see Emma walking towards the villa, clutching her artwork and smiling into the evening air. "I've had the best session EVER," she declared. "I think Lisa was with me in that studio tonight."

THE NIGHT BEFORE THE
GATHERING

$\mathcal{M}$aria stood at the kitchen counter, polishing a stack of wine glasses she wasn't entirely sure they'd need. Her hands moved automatically—wipe, turn, inspect—but her thoughts refused to stay in any one place.

It was past six o'clock. Outside, the garden glowed with that particular honeyed light that seemed to last forever in Spain. A cicada thrummed somewhere near the bougainvillea. The villa smelled of lavender and the faint tang of lemons Rosie had sliced for tea.

She set the last glass on the shelf and pressed both palms flat against the cool tiles. There was a tightness in her chest that had nothing to do with exhaustion.

Part of her longed for the ordinary rhythm of her old life—the certainty of knowing what each day required, what each hour would hold. But standing here, in this kitchen filled with memories and new possibilities, she wondered how she could ever go back to a life so carefully measured.

From the doorway, Emma's voice floated in, gentle but edged with something Maria recognised: quiet determination.

"I've decided," Emma announced, "that I'm keeping the studio in Sóller."

Maria turned, surprised. "The one you've been renting by the week?"

Emma nodded. She stepped into the kitchen, a sketchbook clutched to her chest. "I can afford it if I pick up more classes at the community centre. And Carmen says there's space in the autumn exhibition."

Rosie appeared behind her, carrying an armful of freshly laundered napkins. "Does that mean you're staying for good?" she asked, her eyes wide.

Emma hesitated. "It means I'm staying for…long enough. I don't want to put a finish line on it."

Maria felt a small, amazed laugh bubble up in her chest. "Emma, that's wonderful."

"It's terrifying," Emma corrected, but her cheeks were pink, her eyes bright. "But every time I think about packing up and going back to England, I feel like I'm suffocating."

Rosie set the napkins on the counter. "Then you shouldn't go."

Emma looked down at her hands. "I keep thinking about Lisa. About how she was never afraid to start over. Even when it meant giving everything up."

"She would be so proud of you," Maria said softly.

Emma met her gaze, and for a moment the kitchen felt suspended in that hush of shared understanding—three women, each in their sixties, trying to become someone braver than they'd been.

Rosie turned to the cupboards. "Right," she said briskly, her voice bright. "I'm making dinner. If we're feeding half the island tomorrow, we need our strength."

Maria watched her gather pans and spoons, grateful for her practical energy. It felt like an anchor—something steady to hold onto.

"Do you need help?" she asked.

"No," Rosie said firmly. "You need to sit. Both of you."

Emma gave Maria a wry look and slid onto one of the stools at the counter. Maria joined her, curling her bare toes over the rung. For a few minutes, they just watched Rosie bustle about—slicing onions, humming tunelessly under her breath, pausing now and then to taste the sauce she was stirring.

It struck Maria, in that small domestic moment, how much she loved them both. How this friendship, stretched across decades and continents, had become the truest thing in her life.

Rosie glanced over her shoulder. "So," she said, her tone deliberately casual. "Have you decided what you're doing?"

Maria didn't pretend to misunderstand. She looked down at her hands. "No."

"Are you leaning one way or the other?"

Maria considered. "Some days I think I'll wake up and realise I've been reckless—throwing everything away for a...a fantasy. Other days, I can't imagine going back."

Emma reached across the counter and rested her fingertips lightly over Maria's wrist. "Maybe it doesn't have to be forever," she said. "Maybe it can just be...for now."

Rosie nodded. "Sometimes that's enough."

Maria thought of Carlos—the way he'd looked at her the night before, his eyes warm and unguarded. The way his hand had felt, steady and reassuring, when she'd confessed her fear of wanting too much.

She swallowed. "He asked me to stay."

Neither of her friends looked surprised.

"And you?" Rosie prompted gently.

"I told him I couldn't decide yet," Maria said. Her voice was very soft. "That I needed time."

"That's fair," Emma said. "You've spent your whole life putting everyone else first. You get to take your time."

Rosie set down the wooden spoon and crossed the kitchen

to where Maria sat. She rested both hands on her shoulders and leaned down so their foreheads nearly touched.

"Whatever you choose," she whispered, "we love you. You don't have to be afraid of disappointing us."

Maria closed her eyes. For a moment, she let herself believe that could be true.

DINNER WAS SIMPLE: pasta with roasted vegetables, a green salad, a bottle of the cheap local wine they'd come to prefer over anything imported. They ate with the doors open to the terrace, the twilight pouring in around them.

After the plates were cleared, Rosie brought out a small cake she'd bought from the bakery in town. "For tomorrow," she said, as though that explained everything.

They each had a slice, the sweetness sticking in Maria's throat.

When they finished, Emma disappeared into her room and returned with a shallow box. "I thought we should look through these," she said.

Inside were all the little mementos they'd collected over the weeks: the photograph of Lisa as a child, the scraps of letters and receipts, the blue ribbon that had held the doctor's note. Maria lifted each piece in turn, studying them as though they might still yield some hidden clue.

"Do you remember," Emma said quietly, "that first afternoon in the garden, when we thought we'd never find anything?"

Rosie nodded. "I remember thinking we were all mad."

Maria smiled faintly. "We were."

"But we did it," Emma whispered. "We found her."

IT WAS LATE when they finally drifted to their rooms. Maria stood in the doorway of her bedroom, watching the others disappear down the corridor. She felt a weight in her chest—a mingling of sorrow and gratitude so sharp she had to press her palm flat over her heart.

When she turned to close her door, she found Carlos standing at the far end of the hall, his expression hesitant.

"May I come in?" he asked.

Maria's voice was steady when she answered. "Yes."

THE GATHERING

$\mathcal{B}$y late afternoon, the villa was full of people, laughter, and the scent of things cooking. Rosie had declared, with cheerful determination, that there was no way she would mark the eve of scattering Lisa's ashes without a proper gathering. So they had cleaned and polished, rearranged every chair and cushion, and laid a long table in the garden under the olive trees.

Maria stood at the kitchen counter, her hands sunk into a bowl of dough. She'd offered to bake, partly out of distraction, partly because she needed to feel useful. Each time she pressed her palms into the soft mound, a little of the day's tension slipped from her shoulders.

Through the window, she could see Emma sitting on the terrace with Carmen and Ana, deep in conversation. Every now and then, Emma would laugh—really laugh—and Maria's heart would tug in her chest. She hadn't realised until this trip how much Emma had been shrinking herself over the years, folding into the corners of her own life. Now she was unfurling again.

A soft scuff of footsteps announced Rosie's return. She came in from the garden, flushed and triumphant, carrying an armload of fresh rosemary and basil she'd bullied out of the elderly man next door.

"He tried to give me a plastic bag," Rosie said, dropping the herbs onto the counter, "as though I couldn't carry it with my own two hands. He practically offered to walk me back like I'm ninety."

Maria smiled. "You are his neighbour now. He's allowed to fuss."

"Fuss all he likes," Rosie said. "As long as he keeps bringing the tomatoes."

She began picking over the stems, her hands busy, her expression soft. In the golden light slanting across the floor, Maria thought she looked years younger—less like someone bracing herself against disappointment, more like a woman who had made peace with wanting more.

"I spoke to Mary again this morning," Rosie said after a moment. "She asked me if I was coming home."

Maria kept her gaze on the dough. "What did you say?"

"That I didn't know," Rosie admitted. "That I'd never planned for any of this. But I couldn't leave without seeing it through."

Maria looked up. "And do you still feel that way?"

Rosie's smile was slow and sure. "I think...I'm beginning to understand why Lisa never wanted to stay in one place. Maybe some of us aren't meant for tidy endings."

BY EARLY EVENING, the guests began to arrive. Carmen brought a basket lined with embroidered cloth, filled with savoury pastries. Miguel followed with bottles of wine, and Ana appeared with a tin of little almond biscuits that tasted of sugar and memory.

Carlos arrived last. He paused in the doorway, as if checking that he was welcome, and when Maria lifted her hand in greeting, something in his face eased.

She watched him weave through the people, stopping to greet Carmen and Ana with the affectionate formality of old friends. When he reached her, he rested one warm hand on the small of her back.

"How are you?" he asked, his voice low.

Maria shook her head, unwilling to lie. "I don't know."

"That's all right," he murmured. "You don't have to."

He let his hand fall away without pressing her further. And that—his quiet, patient respect—made her want to curl her fingers into his shirtfront and never let go.

THEY CARRIED platters out to the garden: olives glistening in bowls, wedges of tortilla, thick slices of Manchego, figs split open and drizzled with honey. Miguel fussed over the wine, explaining the vineyard in detail, and Rosie listened with an expression of fond exasperation.

Emma had set up her sketchbook on the far end of the table. Every now and then, she would lift her pencil to capture a gesture or the bend of a wrist. Maria suspected she was working on something she hadn't shown them yet.

Conversation rose and fell in comfortable waves. The neighbours asked polite questions about the scattering planned for the next day. Carmen shared a memory of Lisa—how she'd come into the community centre one afternoon, trailing three children behind her like ducklings, determined to help them find books in English. Maria hadn't heard the story before. She pressed a napkin to her lips as Carmen described Lisa's fierce protectiveness, the way she'd insisted they each have a story of their own to take home.

"She was like that," Maria whispered. "She always wanted to save everyone."

Carmen nodded. "Sometimes it is the ones who feel least saved themselves who most want to rescue others."

Maria had to look away, blinking hard.

As DUSK SETTLED, candles were lit—fat white columns Rosie had found in the market, each set in a chipped glass jar. Their flames wavered in the warm air, casting a hush over the garden.

For a long time, no one spoke. It felt as though the shadows had grown thick with Lisa's presence—her laughter, her impossible optimism, the places she had left herself behind.

Rosie lifted her glass then. "To Lisa," she said simply. "For teaching us how to be braver."

Everyone lifted their own glasses. Maria felt the warmth of Carlos's hand finding hers under the table.

"To Lisa," she echoed.

Emma's voice was softer. "And to the part of her that is still here."

They drank, and the silence that followed was gentle.

After the toast, people began to drift toward the kitchen. Maria stayed behind, sitting very still, watching the flicker of candlelight across the tablecloth. She felt emptied out—scraped clean in a way that was both tender and frightening.

She didn't notice Carlos had returned until his shadow fell across her lap.

"May I sit?" he asked.

She nodded.

He lowered himself onto the bench beside her, close enough that she could feel the heat of him.

"I've been thinking," he began, his voice quiet, "about what you said last night."

Maria closed her eyes.

"I don't want to push you," Carlos went on. "I don't want to be another person asking you to be sure of things you can't be sure of."

Maria turned her face toward him, searching for any trace of disappointment.

He smiled, small and soft. "But I also want you to know this: I'm not going anywhere."

Tears prickled behind her eyes. "That's the problem," she whispered. "You're so good. And I...I don't know if I deserve it."

"You deserve everything," he said.

She made a helpless noise in her throat.

He reached up and cupped her cheek, his thumb brushing the corner of her mouth. "If you want me, I'm here," he murmured. "If you need time, I'll wait."

Maria pressed her lips to his palm, breathing in the steady, warm scent of him.

"All right," she said. "I'll try."

"That's all I ask."

INSIDE THE VILLA, Rosie had put on music—some old Spanish ballad that Maria suspected she'd chosen simply because it made her feel brave. Emma was standing near the fireplace, showing Carmen her sketchbook. Maria crossed to join them just as Emma turned to a new page.

It was the three of them—Rosie, Maria, Emma—sitting together at this very table, their heads inclined toward each other, the candles burning low. The likenesses were imperfect, but the feeling was exact: the hush, the love, the weight of everything they had carried.

Maria touched Emma's shoulder. "You must keep painting," she said fiercely. "Even if you go home someday. Even if you think no one cares."

Emma swallowed. "I will."

. . .

WHEN THE LAST GUESTS LEFT, the villa felt impossibly quiet. Maria stood by the door, watching the lanterns bob away down the drive. Rosie came up beside her, slipping an arm around her waist.

"We did it," Rosie said softly.

"Yes," Maria whispered. "We did."

LATER, when Emma had gone to bed and Rosie was rinsing plates, Maria stepped out onto the terrace alone. The stars were crisp and bright overhead. She felt raw and grateful all at once.

From the kitchen came the sound of Rosie humming—a lullaby she'd used to sing when Mary was small. Maria let it wrap around her like a benediction.

Tomorrow night they would prepare to scatter Lisa's ashes in the olive grove. Tomorrow night, they would prepare to say the last words that needed saying.

But tonight, they were here—safe, loved, alive in a way she hadn't dared to imagine.

And maybe, she thought, that was enough.

THE NIGHT BEFORE

The morning dawned clear and impossibly blue, the kind of day that felt like a gift you hadn't dared ask for.

Maria opened her eyes to birdsong and the hush of the villa breathing around her. For a moment, she forgot where she was. Then she remembered: the olive grove, the letter in her suitcase, the urn waiting on the mantel.

Today was the day.

Not the scattering itself, not quite. But the day they would gather everything they needed—the stories, the mementos, the courage. The day they would ready themselves to say goodbye.

SHE DRESSED SLOWLY, choosing the soft linen dress she'd bought in Palma with Rosie and Emma the week they arrived. It felt right to wear something simple, something she loved.

In the kitchen, she found Rosie already at the table, a mug of coffee cupped in her hands. She looked up with a smile that was tender and a little sad.

"Sleep well?"

Maria nodded. "You?"

Rosie let out a soft laugh. "I dreamed we were back in the university library. Lisa was trying to convince me that we should run off to Paris instead of revising."

"That sounds about right," Maria said, easing into the chair across from her.

They sat in companionable quiet. The kitchen smelled of coffee and warm tiles and the faintest trace of rosemary drifting through the open window.

"Is Emma up yet?" Maria asked eventually.

Rosie nodded toward the garden. "She's been out there for an hour. Sketching."

Maria glanced through the window. Emma was sitting cross-legged on the low wall at the edge of the terrace, her hair unbound around her shoulders, a large canvas propped against her knees.

"She says she wants to finish something before tomorrow," Rosie murmured. "Something she can leave in the grove."

Maria felt her throat tighten. "That's beautiful."

"Lisa would have loved it," Rosie said softly.

By MIDMORNING, the villa had settled into the hush of preparation.

Emma continued to work in the garden, her brush moving in quick, sure strokes. Rosie moved through the rooms gathering things—fresh flowers to carry, the bright scarf Lisa had given her, a little tin of sandalwood incense they'd bought in Sóller.

Maria found herself in her own room, kneeling beside her suitcase. She lifted out the doctor's letter, smoothing the paper flat.

There was something comforting about the weight of it in

her hands. Proof that Lisa had belonged somewhere. Proof that she'd been loved, even before she'd come into their lives.

She set the letter beside her scarf. She would take them both to the grove tomorrow.

IT WAS NEARLY noon when Carlos arrived.

He knocked gently on the open door before stepping inside, carrying a paper bag that smelled of bread and olives and something sweet.

"I thought you might forget to eat," he said.

Maria felt her heart catch. "Thank you," she said simply.

He set the bag on the kitchen table and looked around. "How are you all?"

Rosie came in from the terrace, her arms full of the flowers she'd gathered. "Solemn," she admitted. "But...ready, I think."

Emma followed, wiping paint from her hands. "Hungry," she added. "So you have perfect timing."

Carlos gave them all a smile and began unpacking the food.

THEY ATE TOGETHER at the long table, the windows thrown open to the garden. The breeze carried in the scent of jasmine and the distant sound of church bells.

No one said much. But the quiet was gentle, threaded through with a kind of reverence.

At one point, Carlos poured Maria another glass of lemonade and brushed his fingers across the back of her hand. She looked up, meeting his eyes, and felt something inside her steady.

AFTER LUNCH, they drifted apart again. Emma returned to her

painting. Rosie disappeared into her room to write something in her journal.

Maria stayed at the table, running her fingertip around the rim of her glass. She felt suspended—like she was hovering between the life she'd known and the life she hadn't quite admitted she wanted.

Her phone buzzed against the tabletop, startling her.

James.

She hesitated. Then she picked up the call.

"Mum," James said, sounding tired. "You're up early."

"It's nearly two here," Maria said.

"Oh." A pause. "Right. Spain."

"Yes."

Another pause.

"I wanted to check in," James said eventually. "Sarah said you haven't been home in months."

Maria closed her eyes, breathing slowly. "I know."

"Are you…staying?"

She didn't answer right away. She could hear Emma's brush tapping against her easel out on the terrace.

"I don't know yet," she said honestly. "But…I think I want to."

James exhaled, the sound of it crackling through the line. "Mum, I just don't want you to get hurt. I don't want you to wake up one day and realise you've built your life around something that isn't real."

"I understand," she said quietly. "But for the first time in a long time, I feel like I'm doing something that's mine."

He was silent so long she wondered if he'd hung up.

"Okay," he said finally. "I don't get it. But…okay."

Maria felt something ease in her chest. "Thank you."

"I'll call again next week," he said.

"I'd like that."

When she ended the call, she felt unaccountably light.

SHE FOUND Emma in the garden, dabbing at her canvas with a cloth.

"Finished?" Maria asked softly.

Emma nodded. "I think so."

Maria looked over her shoulder.

The painting showed the olive grove—the old trees twisted and silver, the grass dappled with light. Three women stood beneath the largest tree, their faces turned away, their hands joined.

"It's beautiful," Maria whispered.

Emma looked down. "It's what this has felt like to me," she said. "A place where we found each other again."

Maria didn't trust her voice enough to answer.

IN THE LATE AFTERNOON, Rosie reappeared in the kitchen with a bundle of cloth tucked under her arm.

"What's that?" Emma asked.

Rosie smiled shyly. "A banner," she said. "For tomorrow."

She unfolded it across the table.

It was a length of cream linen, hand-stitched in blue thread.

For Lisa. For love. For every story worth telling.

Maria pressed her hand to her mouth.

"It's perfect," Emma whispered.

Rosie's eyes shone. "I thought we could hang it from the olive tree."

Maria nodded, unable to speak.

THEY SPENT the evening preparing everything.

Rosie arranged the flowers in a wide shallow basket. Emma wrapped her painting in brown paper and tied it with twine. Maria folded the scarf and the letter into a small box.

There was something ritualistic about the work—something that made it feel like a sacrament.

When the last light faded, they sat on the terrace with mugs of chamomile tea, too wrung out for wine.

"Do you remember," Rosie said after a long time, "the night Lisa decided she was going to learn Italian because she thought it sounded sexier than French?"

Emma laughed softly. "And she quit after a month because she said all the verbs were too demanding."

Maria smiled, her throat thick. "But she kept the phrasebook on her bedside table for years."

"Just in case," Rosie said.

They fell into silence again, memories surfacing like bright fish in dark water.

The time Lisa had smuggled a stray kitten into their student flat and insisted it could stay "just until it found its confidence."

The weekend in Cornwall when she'd convinced them to swim in the freezing sea, declaring it would "build character."

The long nights after Maria's divorce, when Lisa had simply shown up with a bottle of wine and refused to leave until the worst of it had passed.

"She was the bravest of us," Emma said again, her voice low.

Rosie shook her head. "She was the most determined. And the most infuriating. But...God, she was wonderful."

Maria wiped her eyes with the heel of her hand. "She really was."

. . .

When the clock in the hall chimed midnight, Emma stood and stretched.

"I'm going to bed," she said. "Tomorrow…is going to be a lot."

Maria nodded. "Sleep well."

Emma bent to kiss her cheek. "You too."

Rosie lingered as Emma disappeared down the hall.

"Maria," she said softly, "are you really thinking of staying?"

Maria looked up. "Yes."

Rosie studied her for a long moment, then smiled. "Good," she said. "You deserve something that's yours."

"So do you," Maria said.

Rosie's eyes glistened, but her smile didn't falter.

When Maria finally went to her own room, she found Carlos waiting in the doorway.

"I didn't want to intrude," he said. "But…I wanted to see you."

She stepped into his arms without hesitation.

"Stay," she whispered.

His hand cupped the back of her neck. "Always."

They didn't talk much as they undressed, as they climbed into bed.

But Maria lay awake long after Carlos had fallen asleep, watching the shadows move across the ceiling.

She thought of Lisa, and the olive grove, and all the endings and beginnings that tomorrow would bring.

And in the quiet dark, she let herself believe that love could be an adventure too.

. . .

THE LAST THING she saw before sleep claimed her was the moon rising over the garden—bright and watchful, like a promise she hadn't known she'd been waiting for.

Tomorrow, they would say goodbye.

But tonight, they were still here. Together.

And that, she thought, was enough.

THE FAREWELL CEREMONY

The morning of Lisa's farewell dawned with a kind of unapologetic splendour that would have suited her perfectly. The sky was as blue as a fresh bruise, the light gilding every leaf, every stone, every hesitant footstep with a brilliance that refused to feel like grief.

Maria woke before dawn. She sat on the terrace, the urn in her lap, and watched the first glimmer of sunlight pour over the rooftops. For the first time since they'd arrived, she felt something close to peace.

When Rosie emerged in a soft linen dress, her hair tumbling loose around her shoulders, Maria saw she had been crying already. But she was also smiling, as though the two things could coexist without contradiction.

"She would have loved this day," Rosie said, her voice husky.

"She'd have insisted on perfect weather," Maria agreed.

Emma was next to join them, carrying a folded note. She looked down at it and swallowed. "I found this in one of her old journals last night. She'd written a list of the places she wanted her ashes scattered. Every single one of them was somewhere she'd had an adventure."

"What was at the top of the list?" Rosie asked.

Emma gave a watery laugh. "Anywhere beautiful. Anywhere my friends remember me."

By ten o'clock, they were at the house with the blue door, standing in the garden as neighbours and strangers gathered in ones and twos. Word had travelled as it always did on the island —quietly, insistently, as if Lisa herself were sending out invitations.

Someone had strung paper lanterns between the olive trees. Tables had appeared laden with baskets of bread and bottles of local wine. A small group of musicians tuned their instruments near the stone wall, the bright notes lifting into the morning like birds.

Carlos greeted everyone with a steady calm that Maria was coming to rely on. He moved from guest to guest, making introductions, collecting stories. When he reached her side again, he held out a glass of orange juice and touched her elbow lightly.

"You don't have to speak if you don't want to," he said softly.

She shook her head. "I think I do. But I'm not sure what words will come."

He smiled. "Then they'll be the right ones."

Emma wandered past, holding the hand of a little girl who shyly offered Maria a fistful of marigold petals. Rosie was talking to Miguel near the doorway, and something in her expression made Maria's chest tighten with recognition. It was the look of a woman who'd thought her heart was closed forever, only to find it unfolding again in spite of everything.

When Rosie caught Maria watching her, she shrugged a little, smiling. "Don't say it," she called across the garden.

"I'm not saying anything," Maria replied.

"You're thinking it, though," Rosie insisted.

Maria lifted her palms in surrender. "Fine. I'm thinking it. And I'm glad."

People began to gather in a loose circle around the old olive tree. Someone passed around small cups of wine. A woman in her sixties with a bright scarf stepped forward first, clearing her throat.

"I didn't know Lisa for long," she began. "But the first time I met her, she was sitting exactly where Maria is now, telling a story about how she once had to hide in the ladies' toilet at a gala dinner because she'd been caught in a scandal with a politician."

Soft laughter rippled through the crowd.

"She said she'd spent forty minutes perched on the cistern, in a sequinned gown, trying to keep her shoes dry. And she was laughing as she told it—like it was the best thing that had ever happened to her."

Rosie covered her mouth, her shoulders shaking. "She called me from that loo," she said when she could speak again. "Said she needed moral support. And a taxi."

Emma wiped her eyes. "She was always in the middle of some chaos."

"And she always made it look like fun," Maria said quietly.

The next speaker was a man Maria didn't recognise—a Spanish gentleman with silver hair and an elegant cane. "I was her doctor in the last year," he said gently. "She came to every appointment with a notebook and a list of questions that made me feel like I was taking an exam."

That drew a collective smile.

"But she was brave. Braver than anyone I've ever met," he continued. "When her health began to fail, she said, 'I am not afraid of dying. I am afraid of leaving things unfinished.' She asked me to promise I would tell her friends that she was grateful. That she knew she was loved."

Maria pressed her palm to her mouth, breathing carefully.

Rosie stepped forward, holding the urn against her chest. "When we were twenty-five," she began, "she made me promise we'd have an adventure every year. Even if it was only to the next town over. Even if it was only for a day. She said adventure was what made life worth it."

Her voice broke.

"And I thought… I thought when she was gone, that would be the end of it. But standing here, with all of you, I realise… this is still an adventure. This whole ridiculous, beautiful journey."

Miguel slipped his hand around hers, steadying her without words.

Emma cleared her throat, her fingers tight around her note. "When she found out she was ill, she sent me a letter. She wrote, 'Promise me you won't go back to living half a life. Promise me you'll make something beautiful out of all this heartbreak.'"

She unfolded the note, her voice barely carrying. "I think… today, we're doing exactly that."

The musicians began a soft, plaintive tune, the melody circling the branches overhead. Maria stepped forward, her hand resting on the urn beside Rosie's.

"She was the bravest person I ever knew," she said. "And the most infuriating. She never let me stay comfortable. She never let me believe I was too old or too settled or too tired for something new."

She looked at Rosie and Emma. "She was my friend. And she was the reason I finally started living again."

Carlos came to stand beside her. He didn't say anything, but his hand settled lightly at the small of her back, anchoring her.

One by one, people stepped up to offer memories. Stories about Lisa's impossible generosity, her wicked sense of humour, her determination to rescue every stray dog she ever encountered. Stories about how she'd cooked for half the street during a power outage, or talked a grieving stranger through the worst night of their life.

When the last of the speakers stepped back, the hush that followed felt almost sacred.

Rosie unscrewed the lid of the urn. The breeze rose and carried a little drift of ash over her hands. She looked at Maria and Emma, her eyes luminous.

"Ready?" she asked.

Emma nodded, slipping her arm around Maria's waist. "Ready."

Maria swallowed. "Let's bring her home."

Together, they tipped the ashes into the grass beneath the olive tree. The breeze lifted them, turned them to silver for a heartbeat, then let them fall among the roots and the scattered petals.

No one rushed. No one tried to fill the silence.

After a long moment, Miguel knelt to gather a small stone from the edge of the path. He placed it gently at the foot of the tree. "For remembrance," he murmured.

Carlos touched Maria's shoulder, and when she looked up, she saw something unguarded and full of hope in his eyes.

"I know this isn't the end," he said quietly. "For any of you."

"No," Maria agreed. "It's the start."

Rosie was leaning into Miguel now, her head tucked under his chin. Emma had her sketchbook out already, drawing the way the light fell through the leaves.

Maria looked around at the faces—some familiar, some she barely knew—and felt her heart expand to hold it all: the grief, the gratitude, the impossibility of saying goodbye.

Someone passed a glass of wine into her hand. Someone else began a low song, and others joined in, until the grove was filled with voices.

Carlos turned toward her. "Will you stay a little longer?" he asked, almost shyly.

Maria felt something lift inside her, a weight she hadn't known she carried. "Yes," she said. "I think I will."

Nearby, Rosie raised her glass in salute, and Maria lifted hers to meet it.

"To Lisa," Rosie called, her voice ringing clear. "The bravest, maddest, most wonderful friend we ever had."

"To Lisa," they echoed, and for a moment, it felt like she was there among them—laughing at all the fuss, shaking her head, delighted that even in death she could orchestrate such a gathering.

As the afternoon deepened, Maria closed her eyes and let the warmth of the sun and the music and the love around her settle into her bones.

She could almost hear Lisa's voice—fond, amused, exasperated and affectionate all at once.

"About time," it seemed to say. "About time you all started living."

And when Maria opened her eyes again, she knew with complete certainty that this was not an ending at all.

It was the first page of something new.

NEW DOORS OPENING

hree months later, Maria stood in the departure
lounge at Palma airport, but she wasn't leaving Spain.
She was seeing Rosie off on what had become a monthly
pilgrimage back to England to sort out the practical details of
relocating a life that had been perfectly organised for
predictability and was now being enthusiastically reorganised
for adventure.

"Are you sure you packed everything?" Maria asked, though
they both knew this was the fourth time she'd asked the same
question in ten minutes.

"I'm sure," Rosie replied patiently. "And if I forgot something,
Miguel will just have to come to England to help me pack properly. He's been threatening to visit anyway—something about
wanting to see the country that produced such excellent
students of Spanish cuisine."

Miguel, who had indeed turned out to express his deepest
feelings through food, had spent the past three months courting
Rosie with a dedication that involved elaborate picnics, cooking
lessons, and what appeared to be a systematic campaign to
prove that life was too delicious to waste on being sensible.

"He's good for you," Maria observed, watching her friend glow with a happiness that came from being adored by someone who understood that love should be both passionate and fun.

"He's ridiculous for me," Rosie corrected. "Completely inappropriate, utterly impractical, and absolutely perfect. Our late friend approved wholeheartedly."

The mention of Lisa no longer brought the sharp stab of grief it once had. Over the past three months, as they had settled into new rhythms and new lives in Spain, Lisa's presence had evolved into something warmer, more comforting, less like loss and more like a blessing that continued to unfold in unexpected ways.

Emma appeared from the café carrying coffee and what appeared to be a small portfolio of artwork.

"Last-minute inspiration," she explained, showing them sketches of the airport scene—travellers saying goodbye, families reuniting, the eternal drama of departure and arrival that played out in places where journeys began and ended.

Emma had flourished in her new role at the community centre in ways that surprised everyone, including herself. Her art classes had become so popular that Carmen had offered her additional hours teaching adults, and her own painting had taken on a vibrancy and confidence that spoke of someone who had finally found her true calling.

"Any word from the gallery in Barcelona?" Rosie asked.

" Galería del Mar in Barcelona wants to include three of my Majorcan landscapes in their summer exhibition," Emma said, trying to sound casual about what was clearly a career milestone.

"Lisa would be so proud," Maria said softly.

"Lisa would be taking credit for the whole thing," Emma replied with a grin. "She'd say she planned the entire Spanish adventure just to help me find my artistic voice."

"Maybe she did," Rosie said thoughtfully. "Maybe that whole

mysterious blue door quest was just her way of making sure we ended up exactly where we needed to be."

It was a theory they had discussed many times over the past three months, usually late at night over wine and a deep conversation that happened when people who had known each other for decades suddenly discovered they were still capable of surprising each other and themselves.

The boarding announcement for Rosie's flight interrupted their philosophical speculation, and suddenly it was time for a goodbye that was both temporary and significant—the first separation since they had arrived in Spain as a unit and were now continuing as individuals who had learned to write their own adventures.

Before Rosie turned to join the boarding queue, she leaned in and hugged Maria tightly, her voice low so only Maria could hear.

"Thank you for being braver than I. For showing me how to start again."

Maria felt her throat tighten. "We did this together," she said, holding her friend just a little longer than necessary.

"Take care of Maria," Rosie said to Carlos, who had arrived with the punctuality of someone who understood that airport farewells required proper attention.

"Take care of yourself," Carlos replied. "And bring Miguel something from England that will make him happy to let you go again."

"I'm bringing him tea," Rosie said solemnly. "He's convinced that English tea is the secret to understanding the English soul. I don't have the heart to tell him it's just leaves in hot water."

The goodbye hugs were fierce and full of love, seasoned with the promise that this was just the first of many hellos and goodbyes, that their friendship had evolved to accommodate distance and change, that love didn't diminish when it expanded to include new people and new possibilities.

After Rosie's plane disappeared into the Spanish sky, Carlos, Maria, and Emma drove back towards Palma through a landscape that had become familiar and beloved. The mountains still took Maria's breath away, the olive groves still spoke of continuity and endurance, and the sea still stretched towards horizons that promised endless possibility.

"How did the EU committee meeting go?" Maria asked as they settled into Carlos's car. "You never told us the final outcome."

Carlos's face lit up with a mixture of relief and pride. "They approved the funding for another three years," he said, reaching over to squeeze her hand. "The committee chairman said your testimony about the personal impact of adoption research was exactly what they needed to understand why the work mattered. You didn't just help me save my career, Maria—you helped me prove that history isn't just about the past, it's about healing the present."

"Fancy dinner at Miguel's restaurant tonight to celebrate? He's been experimenting with a new paella recipe that he claims will make us weep with joy."

"Everything Miguel cooks makes Rosie weep with joy," Emma observed. "I think she's easy to please when it comes to food made with love."

"Some people are easy to please when it comes to anything made with love," Carlos said, glancing at Maria with a smile that still made her heart sing after three months of steady courtship.

Their relationship had developed with the same organic unpredictability that had characterised their entire Spanish adventure. Carlos had courted her with history lessons and long walks through ancient streets, with introductions to local customs and patient translations of bureaucratic requirements, with a steady affection that made daily life feel like a gentle adventure.

Maria had moved into a small flat near the cathedral, close

enough to Carlos's museum that they could share morning coffee and evening walks, independent enough that she maintained her own space and identity. They had learned each other's rhythms, discovered compatible quirks, and built the foundation of something that felt both brand new and completely natural.

"Any regrets?" Emma asked as they reached the outskirts of Palma, the question casual, but the attention to the answer clearly genuine.

"About leaving England?" Maria considered this seriously. "I regret leaving my garden. I regret not learning Spanish before I was sixty-four. I regret waiting so long to discover that I'm braver than I thought I was."

"But no regrets about the big things?"

"No regrets about the big things," Maria confirmed. "What about you? Any second thoughts about staying?"

"Only every other day," Emma admitted cheerfully. "Usually when I'm trying to explain something complicated in Spanish and realise I'm gesturing like a demented windmill. But then I go to the community centre and see what the children have painted, or I finish a landscape that actually captures what I was trying to express, or I remember what it felt like to live a life that was safe but not really alive, and I know I'm exactly where I need to be."

They had become an unlikely trio—the English historian's assistant who had discovered she loved teaching practical skills, the retired librarian who had found her artistic voice through Spanish light and emotional honesty, and the Spanish curator who had learned that some of the best historical discoveries happened when you opened your heart to the present moment.

The community centre had become their unofficial headquarters, the place where their separate lives intersected and their joint mission of honouring Lisa's memory continued to evolve. Maria volunteered in the archives, helping to catalogue photographs and documents from the centre's history. Emma taught art classes and worked on her own paintings in a studio space that Carmen had carved out of a former storage room. Carlos provided historical context for the centre's educational programs and had become something of an expert on the intersection of personal memory and community history.

Together, they had created a small memorial garden in one corner of the olive grove, where a bench bore a brass plaque that read: "In memory of Lisa, who taught us all so much..." The bench had become a favourite spot for quiet contemplation, marriage proposals, and important conversations that required the presence of ancient trees and the blessing of a friend who had learned to watch over them from a place beyond worry.

As they pulled up to the community centre, where Emma would spend the afternoon teaching a workshop on painting landscapes that told stories, Maria felt the familiar swell of gratitude for the series of accidents and intentions that had brought them to this point.

"Same time tomorrow?" Carlos asked, kissing her goodbye with the casual affection of someone who knew that tomorrow was both promised and precious.

"Same time tomorrow," Maria agreed, though they both knew that the beauty of their new life was its capacity for pleasant surprises and unexpected adventures.

Inside the community centre, the familiar sounds of children's laughter and adult conversation in multiple languages created the background music for lives being lived with purpose and joy. Maria settled at her desk in the archive room, surrounded by photographs and documents that chronicled decades of children finding families, families finding healing, and communities finding ways to care for their most vulnerable members.

She was cataloguing a collection of letters from adoptive families—updates and photographs sent over the years to maintain a connection with the place where their children's stories had begun—when she found an envelope that made her stop breathing.

The return address was in English. The name was Margaret Ashworth. The postmark was from fifteen years ago.

With trembling hands, Maria opened the envelope and found exactly what she had somehow expected to find—a letter from Lisa's adoptive mother to Pilar, along with a photograph of Lisa at her university graduation, radiant with a joy that seemed to light up everything around her.

The letter was brief but heartbreaking:

Dear Pilar,

I hope you remember me—I visited several years ago asking about my daughter Lisa, who lived at your children's home in the 1960s. You were so kind to share your memories with me.

I wanted to send you this photograph of Lisa—Lisa, as she chose to be called—at her university graduation. She studied literature and art history, and she's planning to travel the world before settling into a career. She's everything we hoped she would become—curious, creative, kind, and completely fearless when it comes to adventure.

I think of your children's home often, and of the love that helped Lisa heal from her early losses. That love made it possible for her to love us, and for us to build the family we all needed.

Thank you for giving our daughter the foundation she needed to become the remarkable woman she is today.

With gratitude and affection, Margaret Ashworth

Maria sat in the quiet archive room, holding the letter that connected Lisa's adoptive mother to the place where their quest had ended, understanding finally that their Spanish adventure had been part of a much larger story—a story of love that transcended time and distance, of connections that endured beyond death, of the mysterious ways that people who needed to find each other somehow managed to do so.

She thought about Lisa's adoptive mother, making her own pilgrimage to Spain years ago, carrying her own grief and her own need to understand. She thought about Pilar, keeping the letters and photographs of children who had moved on to other lives but remained forever in her heart. She thought about the community centre staff, who continued the work of helping children heal and families form, creating the conditions for love to grow in places where loss had left empty spaces.

And she thought about Lisa whose death had launched them on an adventure that had ended up being about life, about love, about the courage to remain open to possibility even when possibility seemed impossible.

That evening, over Miguel's latest culinary masterpiece (which did indeed make them weep with joy, though that might have been as much about the company as the paella), Maria shared the letter with Carlos and Emma.

"So Lisa's mother came looking too," Emma said softly. "She had the same need we had, to understand the beginning of the story."

"And she found the same thing we found," Carlos observed. "That love, once given, creates connections that last forever."

"I think," Maria said, raising her glass of wine to catch the candlelight, "that Lisa would be very pleased with how her story turned out."

"All of our stories," Emma corrected. "Lisa's, her mother's, Pilar's, ours. They're all part of the same story, really. Different chapters in the same book about how love finds ways to continue itself."

Three hours later, as they walked through the narrow streets of Palma towards their respective homes, Maria realised that she was happier than she had ever been in her life. Not because everything was perfect, but because everything was real. Not because she had avoided pain, but because she had learned that pain could coexist with joy, that loss could become the foundation for new kinds of love, that endings could transform into beginnings if you were brave enough to let them.

"Good night, my dear friends," she said at the corner where their paths diverged.

"Good night, Maria," Emma replied. "Sweet dreams, and see you tomorrow."

"Until tomorrow," Carlos added, kissing her hand with the old-world gallantry that never failed to make her feel cherished.

As Maria walked the final few blocks to her flat, past the cathedral where bells chimed the hour, past the narrow balconies and the small shops and cafés that had become the landscape of her new life, she felt Lisa's presence as surely as if her friend were walking beside her.

Thank you, she said silently to the Spanish night, to the friend whose death had taught them how to live, to the mystery that had led them exactly where they needed to be. For the adventure. For the answers. For showing us that some doors only open when you're ready to walk through them.

Above her, the stars wheeled in their ancient patterns, and somewhere in the distance, a church bell chimed midnight—the end of one day, the beginning of another, the eternal rhythm of time moving forward while love remained constant.

Maria climbed the stairs to her flat, where photos of her Spanish life shared space with memories of her English past, where letters from Rosie described the complicated joy of relocating a heart that had learned to love in multiple languages, where sketches from Emma captured the light that had transformed all their lives.

Tomorrow would bring new adventures, new challenges, new opportunities to choose courage over comfort, love over fear, possibility over predictability. But tonight, she was exactly where she belonged—in a story that honoured the past while embracing the future, in a happiness that came from learning that some journeys led not to destinations but to transformations.

It was, she thought as she turned off the lights and settled into sleep, an ending that was really a beginning.

As they walked back towards the bus stop, Maria smiled for reasons that had nothing to do with their quest and everything to do with the memory of kind eyes and gentle hands and the possibility that some stories were just beginning.

That evening, as Maria sat on the villa's terrace reviewing the day's emotional discoveries, her phone rang. The caller ID showed her son James's number, and Maria felt her stomach tighten with the familiar anxiety that came with unexpected calls from her children.

"Mum, finally," James said without preamble. "I've been trying to reach you for days. We need to talk."

"Is everything all right?" Maria asked, though the tone of his voice suggested that whatever this conversation was about, it wasn't going to be pleasant.

"That depends on your definition of all right," James replied with the kind of forced patience that suggested he'd been rehearsing this conversation. "Sarah told me you're planning to stay in Spain indefinitely. Is that true?"

Maria felt heat rise in her cheeks, though whether from anger or embarrassment, she wasn't sure. "I'm exploring my options."

"Mum, you're sixty-four years old. You don't speak Spanish. You've been divorced for less than two years. Don't you think this whole Spanish adventure is a bit... impulsive?" "Impulsive?" Maria repeated, her voice carrying more edge than she'd intended. "Running off to a foreign country with no real plan, spending money on God knows what, talking about staying permanently when you have a life here-yes, I'd call that impulsive." "James," Maria said carefully, "what exactly is it that you think I should be doing instead?"

"Coming home. Acting your age." His voice softened slightly. "Look, Mum, I understand that the divorce was difficult, and losing Lisa was devastating. But hiding in Spain isn't the answer."

Maria rubbed at her temples, feeling the evening pressing in on her.

"I'm not hiding," she said, though she wasn't entirely sure that was true. "I'm living." "You're running away from reality. And now Sarah tells me there's some Spanish man involved? Mum, you're being taken advantage of. These Mediterranean men, they see older English women with money and-"

"Stop." Maria's voice was sharp enough to cut through her son's protective indignation. "Stop right there."

The silence on the other end of the line was so complete that Maria wondered if the call had dropped. Around her, the Spanish evening continued its gentle theatre-Fernando the peacock strutting through the garden, church bells chiming the hour, the scent of jasmine carried on warm air that felt like a blessing.

"James," she said finally, "I need you to listen to me very carefully. I am not a naive old woman being taken advantage of by a charming foreigner. I am not having a breakdown or running away from reality. I am, for the first time in decades, living a life that feels authentically mine."

"But Mum-"

"No. It's my turn to talk." Maria stood, pacing to the edge of the terrace where the view stretched towards mountains that glowed purple in the twilight. "For thirty-two years, I made decisions based on what was best for your father, what was best for your children, what was expected of a woman my age and circumstances. I was a good wife, a good mother, a sensible person who never took risks or caused problems." "And there's nothing wrong with that," James said, though his voice had lost some of its certainty. "There's nothing wrong with it," Maria agreed, "but there's nothing particularly right with it either. I was safe, James. I was appropriate. I was utterly, completely miserable."

The words hung in the air like a revelation, true in a way that surprised even Maria. She had been miserable-not dramatically, not obviously, but with a quiet, persistent sadness that came from living a life that fit everyone's expectations except her own.

"I didn't know," James said quietly.

"Of course you didn't know. I didn't want you to know. But Lisa's death, and finding her story, coming to Spain, meeting people who have shown me what it means to live courageously's taught me that life is too short for playing it safe."

"And this Spanish man? Carlos?"

Maria felt her heart warm unexpectedly at the mention of his name, the way it had been doing for days now whenever she thought about his smile, his gentle hands, the way he looked at her as though she were someone worth knowing completely. "Carlos is a good man," she said simply. "He's kind, intelligent, and passionate about his work. He makes me laugh. He makes me feel interesting and capable and... alive in a way I'd forgotten was possible." "Are you in love with him?" James asked, and there was something vulnerable in the question that reminded Maria he was still her little boy, even at thirty-eight.

"I might be," Maria admitted. "It's terrifying and wonderful and completely inappropriate for a woman my age, and I wouldn't trade the feeling for anything."

Another silence stretched between them, filled with the sound of Spanish evening and the weight of a conversation that was changing their relationship in real time. "

The house," James said finally. "What about the house? The buyers are getting impatient, and if you're not coming back..."

"I'll make decisions about the house when I'm ready to make decisions about the house," Maria said firmly. "Right now, I'm making decisions about my life."

She crossed to the terrace rail, steadying herself with a hand on the warm stone.

"And Dad? He's been asking about you. I think he's having second thoughts about the divorce."

"Your father is having second thoughts because he's discovered that divorced men our age don't have as many romantic options as they expected, and he's realising that taking care of himself is more work than he anticipated."

"That's not fair."

"It's completely fair," Maria said, though without anger. "Your father left our marriage years before we actually divorced. He's just now noticing because he has to do his own laundry."

"So that's it? You're just going to abandon everything here for some Spanish fantasy?" The question stung because it contained just enough truth to be dangerous. Was she abandoning everything? Was this Spanish life just an elaborate fantasy that would collapse the moment reality intruded?

"James," she said carefully, "I need you to understand something. I spent my entire adult life building a life that looked successful from the outside-stable marriage, lovely home, well-raised children, proper social connections. And it was all real, all meaningful, all worth doing. But it was never mine."

"What do you mean?"

"I mean, I never chose any of it based on what would make me happy. I chose it based on what would make other people comfortable, what would meet other people's expectations, what would prove I was a good enough wife and mother and woman." Maria's voice grew stronger as she spoke, as if the words were clarifying something she'd only half understood. "This Spanish life-it's the first life I've ever chosen purely because it makes me happy." "And if it stops making you happy?"

"Then I'll make different choices. But they'll still be my choices, based on what I want rather than what I think I should want."

By the time they hung up, Maria felt drained but oddly liberated, as if she'd finally said aloud things she'd been thinking for years without realising it.

Maria stood on the terrace for a long moment after she hung up, letting the evening quiet her racing thoughts. The sky above Majorca was a deep indigo, scattered with stars. She thought of Lisa—how she'd insisted there was more to life than playing it safe, how she'd sent them on a journey none of them could have predicted.

Inside, the phone was silent again, and Maria realised she wasn't afraid. For the first time in her life, she trusted herself to know what came next.

She turned back into the villa, feeling the warmth of tomorrow already waiting. There would be morning coffee with Carlos, new classes with Emma at the community centre, calls from Rosie about Miguel and packing up her old house in England.

And there would be her own quiet, everyday joys: the way the bells marked the hours, the smell of baking bread from the café across the square, the knowledge that she had finally claimed a life that was entirely hers.

She lifted her glass toward the empty chair beside her. "Thank you," she whispered. "For everything."

Somewhere in the darkness, a peacock called out, and Maria smiled. Some stories, she thought, never really ended. They just found new ways to begin.

What to know more?
You can pre-order the next book now!
SEASONAL SASSINESS has the answers to all your questions – what happened between Maria and Carlos? Did she move back, or is she still in Spain? Have her children forgiven

her? What about Rosie? Is she with Miguel, or back with her husband Derek, or has she reunited with Mike, the doctor she was with in book one? Will they be back in England for Christmas? Did Emma make it as an artist?

My Book

SEASONAL SASSINESS

Out on 27th November...

When sixty-something Maria and her fabulous sassy sixties housemates finally buy their dream home, they're ready for the picture-perfect Christmas they've always longed for: glittering lights, scandalous Secret Santa gifts, mountains of mince pies, and just a small river of Baileys running through everything.

What they're not ready for? Maria's ex-husband turning up unannounced, wearing a sharp suit, a smooth smile, and carrying a solicitor determined to claim what he says is rightfully his. Suddenly, festive cheer turns to high-stakes chaos, as the man Maria thought she'd left behind threatens to take everything: their home, their savings, and the future they've dared to build.

As snow falls and village gossip spreads like wildfire, Maria faces questions she thought she'd already answered: Will Carlos stand by her if everything falls apart—or was their Spanish romance never meant to last? Will Rosie's Miguel really come for Christmas, or is her summer fling already over? And when Emma's art career finally takes off, can she find the courage to believe she deserves happiness too?

Between Maria's fierce determination, Emma's infectious optimism, and a house full of women who refuse to be underestimated, the Sassy Sixties Club are about to prove that family isn't about blood—it's about who shows up when it matters most.

Full of secrets, second chances, scandal and joy, *Seasonal Sassiness* is the ultimate feel-good festive read—proving that life (and love) doesn't stop at sixty...it just gets far more interesting.

Perfect for anyone who believes Christmas should always come with extra laughter, extra brandy, and absolutely no guarantees of a drama-free holiday.

My Book

Printed in Dunstable, United Kingdom

76913665R00097